PUFFIN B

The WHISPERLING

The WHISPERLING

HAYLEY HOSKINS

PUFFIN

PUFFIN BOOKS

UK | USA | Canada | Ireland | Australia
India | New Zealand | South Africa

Puffin Books is part of the Penguin Random House group of companies
whose addresses can be found at global.penguinrandomhouse.com.

www.penguin.co.uk
www.puffin.co.uk
www.ladybird.co.uk

First published 2022

001

Text copyright © Hayley Hoskins, 2022
Illustrations copyright © Kristina Kister, 2022

The moral right of the author and illustrator has been asserted

Set in 13/18pt Baskerville MT Std
Typeset by Jouve (UK), Milton Keynes
Printed and bound in Great Britain by Clays Ltd, Elcograf S.p.A.

The authorized representative in the EEA is Penguin Random House Ireland,
Morrison Chambers, 32 Nassau Street, Dublin D02 YH68

A CIP catalogue record for this book is available from the British Library

ISBN: 978–0–241–51450–4

All correspondence to:
Puffin Books
Penguin Random House Children's
One Embassy Gardens, 8 Viaduct Gardens, London SW11 7BW

For Mum and Dad

They surround us.

They are as much part of this life as the elements.

They are in the breeze that brushes your cheek, the first call
of birdsong, the shimmer of heat from the sun.

They are in the empty chair in your parlour, that spare seat
in your hansom cab. They are under your bed.

That movement in the gloom? It is them.

Unexplained creaks, mysterious footsteps? Them.

The shiver on your neck that causes you to turn?

The time you thought yourself not quite alone?

You weren't.

They are always here, close by, watching.

Waiting.

Don't be scared.

ALDERLEY

THE YEAR OF OUR LORD 1897

My parents are in the business of death; that is, they run a small undertaker's practice in the village of Alderley where we live, half a day's carriage ride from Bristol.

My pa, a cabinet maker by trade, fashions simple caskets. Mama lays out the bodies. 'The dead can't hurt us' is a much-used phrase of hers.

On the whole, she is right.

The door between our parlour and the small 'dressing room' is rarely locked and my mother's practical approach means death holds little fear for me. The dank sheen of a body in the hours after passing would turn the stomach of many; city folk pay handsomely for potions and powders to stop the body stinking when the rot sets in. I don't know

3

what the fuss is about. If, like me, you've washed and tidied and cared for a body after death, you know it's a vessel; nothing more. Something for your spirit to get around in, so it can live and love and experience all the good and all the bad . . . and then you die and all that's left is a clammy, stiffening carcass.

When you're dead, you're dead.

When you're gone, you're gone.

Unless, of course, you're not.

And that's where I come in.

'Lardy or Battenberg or iced bun or lardy or Chelsea bun or lardy or –'

'Fine, we'll have a lardy!' I say. 'Lardy, lardy, lardy!' I laugh and nudge Sally hard in the ribs with my elbow.

'Ow! Look at them, though, Pegs! Ain't they proper lush?' She has her nose to the baker's window, clouding the glass with every out breath. She grins, wiping the smudge ineffectually with her sleeve. She isn't wrong. Mr Sweeting and his wife have outdone themselves today. Their display is always a treat early on a Saturday morning, when the weekday necessities of warm, crusty loaves and fat, brimming pies are complemented by the most wonderful cakes, buns and pastries.

Alderley is popular with visitors, with its riverside walk, picturesque ruins and a tearoom or two. The village is a pretty place, a necklace of shops and houses threaded along a gently curling river, looping up into wooded slopes and farmland. Our house is on Bothwick Hill, which is a pleasing walk for those that have the time. The track leads you up and up, past the school and vicarage, until, red-faced and puffed, you reach the top, where you can stop in the shadow of St Mary's Church and enjoy a view of the village below. On a clear day you can see for miles, and whenever I'm feeling lonesome I fancy I can see Clifton Lodge and give Sally Hubbard a wave. It's where she works in service, as lady's maid to her mistress, Lady Stanton. I've only seen the house in a photograph, a handsome place, tucked away behind a drive lined with feather-shaped trees, but I can imagine Sally there all the same, going about her chores with a cheerful, tuneless whistle.

Today is Sally's one day off a month, and we are spending it together, or at least part of it. We'll make the most of it, and this means lardy cake.

Sally wears her uniform even on her days off, albeit without an apron, but I don't question it. She's walked taller since taking up her position at the Lodge, and what sort of friend would I be if I knocked the shine off that? They don't have much, the Hubbard family, and, other than her Sunday best (which she won't be wearing today, on account of it being a Saturday), her high-neck, black cotton work dresses are the neatest clothes Sally has.

'I'll get it,' she says, and marches in with a 'Mornin', Mr Sweeting, can I have a lardy, please?', her coil of long red hair bobbing at the back of her head as she goes. I watch her through the fogged-up window, pink tongue-tip set in the corner of her mouth as she decides which lardy she wants, while Mr Sweeting waits patiently with a paper bag held open in readiness. 'That one at the front . . . No . . . Left . . . Yes! Ooh, lovely! How's yer ma? Is she any better?'

'Not so good, Sally love, but thanks for asking. How's your lot? Your pa . . . OK?' He hesitates, as everyone does, when he asks about Sally's father.

'Oh, you know, mostly drunk, but Ma says at least she knows his whereabouts when he can't even find the front door without fallin' over!'

'Oh. Every cloud . . .' says Mr Sweeting, smiling awkwardly as he folds the paper bag tightly round the cake. Sally peals with laughter, seemingly unaware that her pa being a drunkard really isn't very funny at all.

There is a poster in the window of the baker's. I know its wording by heart – we all do, for by law one must be displayed in every public building and every shop, office, inn or place of worship, a reminder that times have changed, that we are modern citizens.

WHISPERLING PROTECTION POLICY:

BY ROYAL DECREE

NO HECTORING.
NO TORTURING.
<u>NO EXECUTING</u>!

ALL INCIDENTS OF THE ABOVE CRIMES
AGAINST WHISPERLINGS ARE TO BE
REPORTED TO A PERSON OF AUTHORITY.

THE PERSON OF AUTHORITY IN THIS
PARISH IS THE REVEREND SILAS TATE.

There was one of these 'incidents' you see, somewhere in a village up north. A young girl was accused of being a whisperling. They tried her, found her guilty; she protested her innocence, but they drowned her anyway.

'Hurry up, Sal!' I glance back at the decree. Whisperlings. Those that can talk to the dead. A flush creeps up my neck.

'All right, all right, keep yer hair on! I got us a big 'un, the very fattest!' She giggles as she dips one hand into the bag and licks a dusting of sugar from her finger. 'You lookin' at that notice again, Peg?'

I shrug. 'I can't stop thinking about that poor girl. If only – oof!' A shove from Sally knocks me fair off my feet.

'*Pfft!* If only what? If only they'd thought to stick up a poster or two!' she scoffs. 'Bleedin' 'eck, Peg, half of the lummoxes that'd do such a thing can't read, an' if they could they'd only grumble about do-gooders forcing them to give up "the old ways". Can't see the point of it, meself. Anyway,' Sal adds, giving me a theatrical wink and waving goodbye to Mr Sweeting, 'there's been no whisperlings – or creepers, if you wants to be rude about them – reported in these parts for decades, has there, babber?'

'Shush, you gommo – someone might hear!' I hiss as we start walking back through the village.

Sally's rosy face is beaming as we link arms, nodding to folk as we pass.

At fourteen, Sal's older than me by two years but you'd never know it. There's a lack of guile about her that makes her appear much younger. Everything is close to the surface with Sally, good and bad. Mama says she's 'young at heart', and that's a perfect way to describe her.

There are others in the village, like Mrs Dulwich, for example, who say Sal is a 'bit soft, like all them Hubbards'. There she is now, white-haired and as brittle tempered as that skinny black cat of hers, lurking behind her potions and unctions in the window of her chemist's shop. It's the last building on the corner before we turn up the hill to home. Inside, the shelves are laden with glass bottles, jewel coloured and stoppered, with a handwritten, white paper label stuck to each one.

'Good morning, Mrs Dul-witch,' we singsong, pausing on purpose between the syllables: discreet but brave enough to make Sally feel better, because this is a small place and Sally has heard what the mean old bat has been saying about her. And then we run, picking up the pace until our chests burn and legs scream, and we laugh and squeal our way past the shopfront and round the corner, until we're safely out of view.

'See 'er starin' at me?' Sally cries, slowing down, and I side-eye her. Her jaw is set and her pretty grey eyes have hardened to lead shots. A Sally storm has rolled in.

'She isn't starin' at you, Sal – she's jus' looking out the window, that's all.' I nudge her playfully in the ribs, trying to blow her clouds away. 'Let's go. You don't want to be causing any trouble, not with your new job and all.'

'She thinks she's better than me, don't she? Because I'm a Hubbard, an' everyone thinks they're better than us.'

'No one thinks that, Sal. Come on now – we've got cake to eat, if you don't squash it first.' I nod at her hands, one gripping the paper bag, the other balled into a fist.

She ignores me, head down, scanning the ground, then dropping to the floor as if to curtsey. She picks up a stone, throws it up and catches it one-handed, bouncing it in her palm to assess its weight. She looks me straight in the eye and shoves the paper bag towards me. 'Here, hold the lardy.'

'I will not.' I fold my arms and twist away from her. 'I'll have no part of this, and if you've got any sense at all in that head of yours you'll put that stone down right this minute.'

'But she deserves it! She's proper horrid and –'

'And what? Throwing a stone through her window will help how, exactly?'

'Well, it'll make her feel bad for a minute, like what she makes me feel.' There's a catch in Sally's voice and for a moment I want to yank the stone out of her hand and lob it myself.

'But what if she gets word to Lady Stanton? You know what she's like, Sal. She's nasty old baggage. Imagine her face, all pinched and pleased with herself if you lost your job because of her. Come on, let's go. Please, Sal.'

Sally sniffs and wipes her nose with the back of her hand, leaving a trail of sugar from the cake glinting on her cheek. 'She said I could go with her to the seaside next time she goes.'

'Who? Mrs Dulwich?'

'No, you lemon, Lady Stanton. She hasn't been feelin' too well and likes the sea air on account of her "constitution", whatever that is. I wouldn't want to miss a trip like that.' She drops the stone.

'Have you ever been to the seaside, Peg?' And, just like that, the clouds are lifted and the knot in my chest unravels. Sally has got *such* a temper, but I can usually pull her out of it.

I link arms with her and drag her towards home before she sees that Mrs Dulwich has stepped out of her shop and crossed the road to watch our progress, hands on her skinny hips, her cat snaking round her ankles.

'No, Sally, I've never been to the seaside,' I reply. 'We'll go when we've made our fortune. That's a promise.'

Minutes later, we sit on my bed and unwrap the lardy cake, tearing open the paper bag and smoothing it flat like a plate. 'Save some for me!' Pa shouted from his usual spot in the parlour as we scurried past, but there's no chance of that.

'This is heaven,' says Sally, shovelling a chunk of cake into her mouth. She's right. It's really good. It's squidgy and gloopy in the middle – if you squeeze it, it oozes with sweet stickiness – and bursting with plump raisins, topped with a crunch of baked sugar. Sal signs her name, *Sally Hubbard*, with her finger in the syrupy paper and I swallow a smile – it wasn't so long ago that she couldn't read a word, let alone write, and now she doesn't miss an opportunity to show off her swirly script. Mama taught her in school and with *hours* of extra lessons at home. Sally tucks half of her share of the cake in its wrapping for later, and we lick our fingers before the syrup trickles to our wrists and rinse our hands in the washbowl in the corner. As I push my hands into the water, a pulse of energy like the buzz of static flashes through me, knocking me back. *What was that?*

'You all right, Peg?' asks Sally.

'Yes, yes, I'm fine,' I say. 'It was nothing, really.'

She's at my side, eyes darting mischievously round the room. 'Ooh, is it a ghost? Is there a ghost here? What they sayin'? They whisperin' at you, Peg? Is it right here?' She pauses, then jumps to one side. 'Or here?'

'Stop it, Sally.'

She grins, then jumps again. 'Here maybe?'

'Sally!' I'm laughing now because she's acting so daft and, whatever it was, it has gone. It's been happening more and more lately, although I've kept that to myself. I'm used to feeling a ripple in the air or a flutter in my chest letting me know a spirit is close by, hesitating for some reason before they move on from this world. I *should* be used to it by now, given it's been happening since I took my very first breath. Except . . . this time it was more than the usual flutter or ripple.

This was a whip-crack.

I probably imagined it. It's likely that poster at the bakery has put me on edge; all the posters have, ever since they started springing up. There's a cloud of suspicion hanging over everyone, and that chills me, for was it not the same with the witches? Anyone odd or difficult was suspected of being one. The harmless old woman who looked a bit funny; the wise-woman who grew medicinal herbs; the poor childless widow who talked to herself; that stubborn girl who wouldn't be tamed . . . Witches, all of them, or so it was decided. That last one gives me the shivers the most.

It became a pastime, witch-hunting, like dancing or scrapbooking. Some whisperlings were killed in those times too, Pa told me, before folk came to their senses and it was put a stop to. Little wonder he tells me to keep my mouth shut: no one can know my secret. Pa says it's best that way.

Sally knows, though. She's known since I was three, when I told her about the 'nice lady with the rainbow round her' who asked if I would remind her husband to 'feed the poxy dog'. She giggled at my potty mouth, but believed me without question. Things are never complicated with Sally, and that's why she's my best friend.

A knock at my bedroom door. 'Peggy, when Sally goes home, there's half a dozen eggs going spare, and a quart of milk that we won't get through before it turns. She'd be doing me a favour taking it.'

'ThankyouMissusDevona,' Sal calls. She has cause to say it so often it's become one word.

'And, Peg,' adds Mama, 'I'll need your help in the dressing room in a bit.'

'Of course, Mama.'

Sally waits until the pad of my mother's feet has reached the stairs. 'Do you know who it is?' she asks.

'The boy from the dairy farm, Barney something or other. Got the consumption, poor lad.'

'I knows him! Ooh, there's a shame. He was a right looker, all tall and strong and fair-haired.'

'I wouldn't know,' I lie, remembering the blush that crept up my neck when I peeked in on him earlier. I can't sense his spirit at all now, which is both a crushing disappointment and a huge relief.

Sally taps her lip with her finger. 'Do you . . . Would you . . . Nah, I can't say it!'

'What? Do I, would I what?'

Sally smiles impishly and nibbles at her thumbnail, her eyes gleaming with devilment. 'Would you sit with him? Hold his hand and pretend he's your sweetheart?'

'Sally!'

'What? Where's the harm?' She rolls back on my bed in delight. 'Go on, I dare you!'

'No!' I say, all the more indignant as I can't honestly say it didn't cross my mind. I'm not sure about boys yet. Mama says there's plenty of time for all that. I look at Sally, flush-cheeked and giggly.

'It's fine,' says Sally. 'You can do it and confess afterwards cos you'll be dissolved of all your sin.'

'It's *absolved*, you banana. What are you talking about though?'

'Oh . . . Mr Tate was at the Lodge in the week. He came to pay his respects to the lady of the house.' She pulls a face. 'But the lady of the house can't stand him. Oh, Peg, the names she calls him when his back is turned! Nothin' very ladylike about them at all!' She grins, then her face falls. 'He's been there a lot lately, whisperin' in Lady

Stanton's ear.' She pauses. 'He was askin' about you again.'

The Reverend Silas Tate. His name makes my skin scuttle. Sally reaches for my hand and squeezes it, tight.

'I know, Peg.'

A pink doll-like splodge appears on her cheeks, deepening in colour as I look at her.

'Sally? What's wrong?' I ask.

'He wanted to know if you'd been up to any of your old tricks.'

'My old . . . What did you say?'

'Nothin',' she says, snatching her hand away and tucking it under her skirts.

'Sally?' Blood thuds in my ears. 'Great greengages, Sally, please say you didn't –'

'I can't lie to a vicar! He might get me sent to hell or somethin'!'

'No, Sally! No, no, no, no, NO! He can't do that – we've been through this! What did you tell him?'

'I said I didn't know what he was talkin' about.'

I relax. 'Well, all right then. That's fine. You had me worried for a minute.'

'But then,' she hurries on, 'he got me all confused an' started askin' loads of different questions an' I got a bit flustered, an' then I think I said that if you *could* speak to dead people – only if you could, mind – then I definitely wouldn't tell him anythin' about it an' folks should mind their beeswax an' not listen to rumours an', besides, if you *could* talk to dead folk, then there's no harm in it an' really it's just a skill – like speakin' French or somethin'.' Her cheeks are scarlet now, as well they might be. How could she be so *stupid*?

'Oh, well done – that definitely put him off the scent, didn't it?'

'I. Didn't. Say. Nothin'. Wrong.'

'Yes you DID, Sally! Why did you have to say *anything*?'

'All right, Miss High and Mighty, don't get yer bloomers in a bunch!' Sally shifts on the bed, shoving the wrapped cake to the floor in a swift, angry motion, her eyes burning. 'YOU weren't there! YOU don't know what he's like –'

I'm on my feet, hands clenched. 'Of course I know what he's like! That's why I stay out of his way!' I boot the paper bag so hard it slams into the wall, the cake Sally's carefully saved for later exploding over the floorboards. 'At least that way I don't have to worry about saying something so bogging STUPID!' I shout.

I want to take it back, straight away. Heavy tears wobble in Sally's eyes and I step towards her, reaching out a hand, but she slaps it away. The heat of her mounting fury is already drying her eyes. 'Don't,' she says. 'Don't you dare.' She gathers her things, scrabbling at her coat and gloves. 'You think you're so special, don't you, Peg?'

'I . . . What do you mean?'

'You with your *gift*.' She sneers at the word. 'But it doesn't make you better than other folks, Peggy Devona, and it definitely don't make you better than *me*! Jus' because your *pa* says you're special doesn't mean everyone else thinks so. You're a really terrible friend. Maybe Mr Tate is right – maybe you are an abominable-ation.'

'Abomin–' I see Sally's fist curl and I bite down on my lip, stopping the urge to correct her. 'If you really think that,' I say, 'then get out.'

She hesitates. I should say sorry, and then *she* will say sorry, and then we will be fine, as we have been a hundred times before.

I say nothing.

Sally turns on her heel, marches out of the room and down the stairs. Mama calls after her but she's gone.

A week goes by. There has been no word of Sally from the Lodge, and her mother was little help when I called by with the eggs and milk that she had forgotten in her haste. I thought that Sally might have left a note or passed me a message through her mother, but there was nothing. Fine, if she wants to be like that. Fine. I really don't care. No odds to me at all. Cowpats to her. She's probably having a jolly old time at the seaside with Lady Stanton. Good for her. I hope she gets her toes nipped by a horde of hungry crabs.

Curse you, Reverend Tate! My fight with Sally is all his fault. Five years ago he ignored me, the small girl who tugged at his sleeve and told him there'd been an accident down the pit. The look that that poor man's spirit gave me will haunt me forever. He used every ounce of energy he had left to give me that message. *Get help*, he'd said, but the vicar dismissed us both. He swatted me away like a fly on his black wool frock coat and has hated me ever since. Would it have made a difference, those minutes that were wasted? Could more lives have been saved?

A noise jolts my thoughts and I slide my book under the coverlet. This morning my insides are cramping again and I reach for the hot stone Mama gave me, but it's long cold. I'm supposed to be doing my chores rather than reading, but all that will happen is that tomorrow I'll have to do them all again, so really, I think, what's the point? Why waste my time dusting, when I could be losing myself in worlds more exciting than my own? . . . There's the noise, again. An insistent *rat-a-tat-tat* at the scullery door, the rattle of glass giving it away. Wolf, always close by, looks up and whines, wet-pebble eyes latching on to mine. I pad to the top of the staircase, the floorboards smooth under my bare feet.

'Mama?'

My mother looks up from where she hesitates at the bottom of the stairs and smiles stiffly. 'Peggy,' she says, 'there you are. I've been looking for you everywhere.'

I am about to question this statement – there are five rooms in our cottage and a thorough search would have taken her no time at all – but something about her ghastly pallor stops me. She wipes her hands on her apron. 'Will you answer the door? There's a good girl.' Her voice is tight and unnaturally high.

'Is everything all right?' I ask, turning my head as the knocking resounds once more. 'Who is it?'

'Mr Bletchley,' says Mama.

I honestly don't know why my mother tolerates him. I know he's family – my father's brother, in fact, though you'd never know it. I will *not* call him 'Uncle' for he is no such kin to me; I'd sooner refer to Mrs Dulwich as Aunty Agnes! Mr Bletchley and I don't even have the same last name, not since the brothers had a mysterious falling-out, after which Mr Bletchley disappeared and wasn't seen in the village again until after the accident at the mine. Imagine being in such a huff with your sibling that you change your own last name! And Mama doesn't trust him, of that I'm certain, and that's good enough for me.

'Can we not hide?' I whisper, creeping down the stairs and putting my head round the parlour door in the hope that Pa agrees with my suggestion, but the room is empty. He too has no wish to see his brother and makes himself scarce whenever he calls. 'Mr Bletchley wouldn't know we were home, what with the lamps not lit and no fire in the grate.'

A pause. A sigh. A sag of shoulders. 'No, Peggy. Show him into the kitchen and offer him some tea. I'll make myself presentable and be through in a moment. Sooner he's in, sooner he's gone.' She's too nice, is Mama.

The outline of his top hat is the first thing I see when I approach the scullery door, every movement causing it to loom ever more terribly through the rippled glass, and for a moment I hesitate, for he's a tall, imposing figure.

A second silhouette, smaller and wider, hat cocked at a ridiculous angle, appears at his side. I am immediately irritated and open the door while trying to smooth my raised hackles.

'Mr Bletchley,' I say, bobbing a reluctant curtsey as he sweeps in. He's likely in his fifties, with a good sweep of hair and a rich man's moustache, for which I'd bet a shilling he has a special little comb he uses to tend to it like a beloved pet. Broad of stature and well fed, in my mind he's always overdressed. Today he wears a black frock coat, grey twill trousers, a swirly-patterned sky-blue waistcoat and matching necktie so voluminous I swear he's tipping his head back to avoid it rubbing his chin. Or maybe, in keeping with the fancy businessman that he is, he's just looking down his nose through his gold-rimmed glasses at us commoners. He ignores me anyway, for a girl of twelve is no longer an amusing child nor yet considered good company.

His colleague follows him: shorter, wider, bumblier. 'Master Chimpwell,' I say, letting go of the door so that it bangs against the younger man's foot.

'SHIPwell,' he corrects automatically, his face flaming as he notices my ill-hidden smirk.

'May I make you some tea, gentlemen?' I say, lifting the copper kettle to the hotplate. It's heavy, but I make every effort not to show it.

'That would be very pleasant, Miss Devona,' replies Mr Bletchley. (Well, what do you know? I am suddenly visible.) 'A capable young girl like yourself would do well in service. Perhaps get out of the village, see a little more of this fine land.' He pauses. 'I may even have a job for you myself.'

My stomach drops. Not this again. My eyes flick to the narrow sideboard on the far side of the scullery, next to the washing dolly and mangle. I pick it out immediately – the business card propped up against a small brass rabbit. It's no bigger than a box of matches, its golden copperplate script glinting against a navy-blue background.

Jedediah Bletchley's Psychic Emporium, it reads. *Communicate with the Other Side! – By Invitation Only.*

There is a telephone number (the man is an insufferable show-off) and, underneath, a symbol: a simplistic eye set in front of what could be the outline of a crown. The eye is presumably there to represent the supposed 'second sight' skills of the clairvoyants in his employ. And the crown? Its only significance is the insight it gives into the man's over-inflated opinion of himself.

It truly baffles me how, not ten miles away, there are people faking the gift that I must hide (for none of them are genuine whisperlings, that is certain). Nowadays, speaking with the dead has become entertainment for the wealthy and terminally stupid. And this man – this *Devona* man – is part of the farce. How *could* he?

Mr Bletchley eyes me curiously, face reddening when he sees what I'm looking at. I wonder, not for the first time, if this is what he and my father fell out about. Was Pa's brother a traitor to our whisperling legacy? I hold Mr Bletchley's gaze for as long as I dare; he looks away first and I swallow a fizz of triumph.

'And where is the fragrant Mrs Devona?' he simpers. 'Not avoiding me, I hope.'

At this, Mama sweeps into the room, her strawberry-blonde hair loosely piled into a cottage-loaf bun, a pencil sticking out of the top. Her features are small and freckled, her skin lightly tanned, and her eyes are greener than jade. Pa sometimes calls her Peachy, which suits her perfectly, though her name is Lydia.

'Mr Bletchley, I do apologize. I had something I had to attend to. I trust Margaret has been attentive?'

'Ah, do not concern yourself, my dear woman. I can assure you that we're being well looked after. I've made mention to Margaret that, given her age, she might like to secure a role in service. I could always speak to one of the local houses, or perhaps she could come to work for me – as always, the offer is there . . .'

'Why, thank you, Mr Bletchley. That's terribly kind of you, but Peg – but Margaret is invaluable to me at the schoolhouse, helping to keep an eye on the younger ones, not to mention helping around here when winter comes and things get busier.'

Mr Bletchley thins his lips. The action nudges loose a bead of sweat, which rolls from his nostril, over his mouth and down to his chin. I look away, for fear of my morning porridge flying up from my stomach. 'Well, if you insist, dear lady, on holding to these modern ideas of education for the masses . . .' A smile plays under his moustache. He is teasing, but my mother glares at him. He catches her look, and his grin disappears under a cloud of disappointment. He looks down at the table and runs a buffed, clean fingertip over the edge as if inspecting for dust. 'I suspect young Margaret here would fancy herself a scholar.'

'Well, *of course* I would!' I say indignantly. To have an education like boys – like *him* (I slide a daggered glance at Ambrose Shipwell) – would be everything.

He will go to university! Even if we had the money I wouldn't be allowed, because I'm a *girl*. It is *infuriating*! I am *far* cleverer than him.

Mr Bletchley looks at Mama, bitter and regretful. 'But for a flip of a coin, eh?'

I'm not sure what he means, but Mama ignores him and looks towards the parlour. I know what she's thinking. *What if Pa heard?*

I grip the kettle handle, feeling its heat through the cloth, and imagine the look on Bletchley's face should I swing the copper from the hotplate and drop it on to his shiny shoes.

But I don't. Mama says that lately we've needed Mr Bletchley, business-wise, and that's why she tolerates his visits. So instead I say, 'Are you happy to take your tea here at the kitchen table, Mr Bletchley, or would you be more comfortable in the parlour? We've only the one body in today and he's reasonably fresh. I mixed some camphor in with the lamp oil, so you probably won't smell anything at all if I light it and keep the door to the dressing room shut.' Then I give him my purest smile as his florid face pales to ash and he grips the edge of the table, knuckles as white as bone.

*

'You're a sharp one, all right,' says Ambrose Shipwell, tugging at the royal-blue cravat under his chin. The smug smile dancing round his lips infuriates me.

'Choking you?' I say.

He squints at me. 'No,' he says. 'It's just a little snug this morning.'

'Perhaps you should lay off them meat pies, Ambrose,' I say, nodding at his rounded belly straining under his flannel trousers. He looks out of place in our little courtyard – so full and ruddy and plump, so resplendent in navy and plum: a loud, colourful shout among the pale-washed whisper of grey flagstones and reedy, long-harvested vegetable beds.

'What does Mr Bletchley want?' I ask.

'The usual arrangement, I imagine,' he says. 'A body from the gaol to tidy up, ready for some scholars to prod and study. A body that no civilized funeral home will deal with.'

I pounce at him, fists clenched. 'And we're considered *uncivilized*, I suppose? Why you –'

'Peggy, stop – that's not what I meant!' Ambrose holds his hands up and backs away. 'You know what city folk are like. It'd be bad for business if they knew their beloveds were sharing a funeral slab with a prisoner who'd been hanged. Your family is discreet and sensible and the pay is good. I know Mr Bletchley has a soft spot for your mother . . . Don't huff, Peggy – he wants to help out.'

'I still can't believe he invested in a city undertaker's. It's like everything he does is to show how much better he is than us. Than Pa.'

'He's the landlord of the undertaker's, nothing more. It could easily have been a sweet shop or a dressmaker's. Not everything is a conspiracy, Peg. And since the mining accident it's obvious he'd want to help you. He's your family, like it or not. Your mother would never accept handouts, so this is one way for him to do it.'

'We haven't had a body from the gaol for ages,' I say carefully. What I mean is we haven't had one for over six months because Mama asked not to be involved any more in that sort of work, money or no money. Ambrose clearly doesn't know this.

He shrugs, then grimaces. 'You know they think they can tell if someone was born evil by what's inside them, or by counting the bumps on their head. Have you ever heard such rot? Excuse the pun!' He giggles. 'They should chuck the lot of 'em in the pit after the long drop, if you ask me. Who in their right mind would want to dig about in a dead convict's innards? The very thought of it turns my stomach.'

I honestly can't say I blame him, even if his reasons are different from mine. If only he knew.

'Although . . .' he continues, 'a dead body is a dead body, wouldn't you say?' He watches for my reaction. 'I mean, it's not like they can *do* anything once they're gone, is it?'

'I'm not sure what you mean,' I say.

Ambrose straightens his hat, meaning business. 'I've heard that sometimes the dead will speak, if they have an accommodating ear to speak to.'

'Well, that sounds very fanciful,' I say, smoothing my skirts. The tops of my legs are aching now, to match the dull throb in my back and stomach. Can't these two leave so I can heat up my stone and take to my bed again? Better still that our places would switch and Ambrose Shipwell could deal with the insufferable monthlies, do my chores, help with the ungrateful brats at the schoolhouse, *and* have it suggested to him that his future lies in servitude.

'Don't be coy, Peggy,' he says. 'It's perfectly acceptable these days to be a whisperling. People like you are rather fashionable in the city. Everyone knows you have the gift. I'll bet that's why Bletchley sends you the *interesting* bodies in case they wish to chatter!'

'Well then, *everyone* is a fool, especially you!' I catch Ambrose's smirk at my outburst and poke my tongue out at him.

I've known Ambrose forever. He had no ma or pa of his own but was adopted by Mr Shipwell, and grew up in one of the bigger houses close to the river. When we were younger we'd spend every summer's day swimming and dunking and launching off the rope swing above the deepest spot by the jetty. It's odd to see someone you've seen in their undercrackers all polished and puffed and playing at being a grown-up. He has long suspected my whisperling abilities, but Pa was jumpy enough about Sally knowing so I kept my counsel, and eventually Ambrose stopped asking. Also, he is a *boy*, and an annoying one at that, so I didn't blab, but even so it's exhausting keeping the secret from him. Now he works for Bletchley it's even worse, but for Pa's sake I continue the charade.

'So, how is business at the emporium?' I say. 'Still scamming unsuspecting folk with your elaborate parlour games?'

'Your reluctance to be truthful about your gift is one thing, Peggy, but your certainty that everyone else is a charlatan is remarkably pompous.' He grins. 'Even for you.'

'Oh please!' I reply.

'Honestly, Peggy! I have seen things with my own eyes that I could scarce believe!' He beams with stupid delight. 'I've seen spirits of the dead transform themselves into solid form, heard voices from a different realm, watched as the ghosts take hold and speak through the living!'

At this I give pause. I don't think he is trying to trick me. 'At the emporium? What do you mean?'

'A spiritualist, Miss Richmond – she has the power to allow her body to be used by those who have passed in order for their beloveds to feel their touch or hear their voice once more.'

'Well, that sounds . . . strange. So you actually saw her *become* the dead person?'

Ambrose hesitates. 'Well, no. She doesn't do that, for surely that would be the work of the Devil.'

'Quite.'

'So she doesn't transform, exactly, but the very essence of the person speaks through her.'

'Oh, come *on*!'

'Well, you obviously don't know about these things, being such a little country mouse,' he blusters. 'But we do. It's not like we're fools, is it?'

I raise an eyebrow. I didn't realize it before, but if you are quiet for long enough you can hear the rattle of someone's irritation. Ambrose is a tittle-tattle toad ready to gobble up gossip. Does he really think he can manipulate me into revealing my gifts?

That said, it doesn't hurt to have a little fun.

'Did I ever tell you, Ambrose, about one of the first cadavers we had from the gaol?' I ask.

'No. What happened?'

I nod towards an upturned pail next to the chicken house. 'Sit down and I'll tell you,' I say, and Ambrose obliges, dragging the pail next to me while I perch on a milk crate and tidy my skirts.

'This feels like a church confessional!' says Ambrose, settling himself down.

I grimace at the mention of church, and an unwelcome image of Mr Tate slithers into my head. I'm more likely to trust the rats that scuttle through the slop trough with my eternal soul than our weasel-faced vicar, but there we are. I take a theatrical breath and begin.

'I knew we were due a body. The cart went by when I was walking up from the village. I'd got some of the butterscotch drops that Pa likes and was about to pinch one, but the sight of that box bouncing around . . . well, it turned my stomach, just thinking about what was jiggling about inside. I half expected the body to bob right out in front of me.'

'Were they from Bailey's?'

'What?'

'The sweets. Were they the ones from Bailey's, the ones with the brown stripe running through? They're the best ones, I think, better than –'

'You wish to discuss the *sweets*? Really, Ambrose! *That's* all you're curious about?'

'I apologize, Miss Devona. Please tell me more about the corpse of the ne'er-do-well.'

I tut at his ridiculous turn of phrase.

'I couldn't sleep that night, knowing that there was such an evil sort lying out downstairs, not ten feet under my head. I'd heard them talking to Mama, the men that brought the body. They said he was a shameless beast who'd laughed when they put the noose round his neck. Imagine that!'

'I'd rather not,' said Ambrose, rubbing at his own neck.

'I must have nodded off eventually, for I woke with a jump. I glanced at the gap at the bottom of my bedroom door, and was reassured to see the glow of lamplight. But then I saw something else. In the middle of the yellow light was a small black patch and it was slowly growing, from the size of an eye at first, to a fist . . . to a foot. I tried to scream but no sound would come, so I watched helplessly as this *thing* slid under my door . . . and disappeared. I held my breath. Had it all been a nightmare? But then came a movement. At the foot of the bed. Under the cover. Ambrose, it was IN MY BED!'

I side-eye Ambrose. He is covering his face with his cravat, the daft dollop.

'Shall I tell you how I escaped from this dreadful creature, Ambrose?'

He nods his head, jaw slack and quavering.

I tap my ankle discreetly and Wolf, responding to my silent signal, brushes Ambrose's leg.

Ambrose shrieks. He tips backwards on the upturned pail, landing in an undignified heap as Wolf slobbers over him, and I roar with laughter.

'Wolf, you scared me so! Miss Devona, that is quite a tale.' He regards me from the flagstones, then turns to scratch Wolf under her chin. She responds by lifting a paw for Ambrose to shake, which he does with much ceremony. It annoys me that Wolf likes this buffoon. I thought dogs were supposed to be good judges of character. 'Have you been playing with me, Peggy?' Ambrose says.

'Course I haven't! How could you suggest such a thing!' I say, leaving him to right himself as I turn away and allow myself a smile. I don't mind Ambrose, not really. Not that I'd ever tell him that. It's nice to have someone to torment, and he'd believe anything, the dozy doorknob.

To be fair to Ambrose, however, my tale wasn't completely fiction: it wasn't one of the first cadavers we'd had, but the very last. 'Everyone has a right to dignity,' my mother had said after that, 'but no more bodies from the gaol.' She told Mr Bletchley so too, in no uncertain terms, which makes me more curious about what today's visit is for. He tends not to drop in without good reason, for my father made it patently clear to him many years ago that he was not welcome.

The clatter of the pail brings Mr Bletchley and my mother to the yard, the former unnaturally stony-faced. Bletchley would describe himself as jolly and charming, so it's unusual to see him this annoyed.

'Quite the commotion out here,' he says, rocking back on his buttoned boots and casting a pitying eye around our garden. 'Nice to see you young folk getting along for a change.' His eyes land on the privy and he pats his stomach. 'Mrs Devona, would you please be so kind as to let me use your, ahem, facilities?'

'Of course,' says Mama. 'I'd be honoured.'

I raise a brow at her obvious sarcasm. I don't know what they've been talking about in there, but it's plainly got to her, as the scarlet flush at her throat attests.

A wave of collective embarrassment at watching a man like Mr Bletchley prepare to do his business sends the three of us back into the kitchen. Mama pours Ambrose and me a cup of milk, pushes a slice of bread and dripping towards Ambrose, and mouths a silent order for me. 'Behave,' it says.

Suddenly a terrible thought occurs to me. 'Oh, Mama!'

'Whatever is it, child?' she says. 'You've gone quite pale. Drink your milk and calm yourself.'

'My . . . my . . .' I glance at Ambrose, but he is shovelling bread into his mouth as if he'll be starved from now until Christmas. 'My rags, Mama!'

'Are they not covered in the pail?' she asks, and I shrug helplessly. I truly can't remember and now my head is spinning with embarrassment. Moments later Bletchley steams in, cheeks red, and clips Ambrose unnecessarily round the ears. 'Come along, lad, stop stuffing your face. You'll not fit into the carriage if you keep on like that. Quick, quick, I don't have all day. Good day, Mrs Devona, Miss Margaret,' and he tips his hat without even looking at us.

'Yes, goodbye, dear ladies,' says Ambrose. 'I'll see you again, perhaps next –' but he is cut off by Bletchley, who grabs his arm, drags him down the path and through the gate. Such is his impatience to leave that I swear if he'd been a fitter man he would have leaped over it.

'Oh, Mama, I'm sorry – I'm so ashamed! What must he think?'

Mother grips my shoulders, the pinch of her fingers bringing me back to the now. I smell the faint, soft warmth of violet cologne and feel her breath on my cheek. As I settle, her grip softens and she pulls me to her.

'There now,' she says, stroking my hair. 'Like as not, he wouldn't know what they were anyway. He has no *Mrs* Bletchley, but if there ever were one she'd never have to deal with her own sanitary napkins. Don't you trouble yourself about it.'

'Of course, I won't do it again. I'll be more careful . . .'

'That's not what I meant,' says Mama, choosing her words carefully. 'What I mean is, this won't be the last time we unsettle men, Peggy, simply by virtue of the fact we're women.'

It has been several days since Mr Bletchley's visit.
I've had no word from Sally and if I'm honest I'm
more than a bit put out. Our spats have never lasted
this long. Usually by now, Sally would have realized
she was in the wrong and said sorry and everything
would be normal again. Except, I know it wasn't
her fault. It's never her fault. Well, hardly ever – she
does have a *stinking* temper.

Mama heard me crying last night. She came into
my room, lay down and put her arm round me, and
I nuzzled my face into her cheek like a baby. She
smells lovely, does Mama, of cold cream and face
powder, and of the cologne that comes in little blue
glass bottles that sit on her dressing table and catch
the light like kaleidoscopes. She suggested I write

Sally a note, as she stroked my hair in the dark, nails gently grazing my scalp, sending tickles of comfort down my back.

It's a good idea. I hope it works.

Dear Sally,

I am a truly diabolical friend. You were right – it wasn't your fault. Mr Tate is an evil old goblin with breath like a butcher's armpit. Please can we forget about it? You were right (again!) – I was being uppity and I'm so sorry about booting your lardy cake. That was a rotten thing to do.

Kindest regards, your BEST (if sometimes TERRIBLE!) friend,

Peggy Devona

PS Saw Ambrose last week. He is still an annoying fopdoodle.

I fold the note into four, carefully seal it in an envelope addressed to *Sally Hubbard, c/o Clifton Lodge, Bristol,* and tuck it away, knowing I'll be as fidgety as a frog on a hotplate until I get a reply.

I confess I find myself jumpier than usual of late. Something dark has been lurking just behind my line of vision, creeping up on me like a sinister game of grandmother's footsteps. My row with Sally unsettled me, of course it did, but it's more than that. Was it the strange visit from Mr Bletchley maybe? Or . . . something else? Something big. Something to do with my gift. If Sally were here, she'd tell me to stop worriting until whatever it is slaps me in the chops, because worriting changes nothing and the sky will fall in on a person whether they've a smile on their fizzog or a grizzle in their guts, so you may as well be happy while you're able. Not having her here to talk sense into me makes me miss her all the more.

But Sally *isn't* here, so whatever it is, whatever is coming, I must carry on without her. Like it or not, I am a whisperling and I can't hide from that – nor would I want to, for on the whole it is a beautiful thing, a privilege even, being there when a spirit leaves. I don't always see it. Sometimes I'm simply not there; sometimes they don't linger at all. But should they wish, and I'm close, they can talk to me if I'm there at the burn.

The burn. It's one of the first things a whisperling learns about. When a person is on the point of death, that's when their spirit is at its most powerful, its most vibrant, like the flame of a freshly struck match.

That's why it's called the burn. Burn bright, burn fast, burn out.

Today is a school day, so there is little time for brooding. I know I'm a bit old for school – the law says you should be schooled until the age of eleven and I've passed that, not that most folk give a turnip about the law when there's coal to mine or crops to pick. We haven't really talked about what work I'm to do, other than *absolutely not* going to work for Mr Bletchley, but if I'm not careful I'll just slip into Mama's shoes. Already I'm helping with the young 'uns – helping them with their reading, filling up their inkpots, and supervising them when they eat their dinner or play in the yard. It could be worse, I suppose, but I also know it could be much, much better.

The school is halfway up Bothwick Hill, above the village and in the shadow of St Mary's Church, which is at the crest of the hill. On a fine day the river looks so pretty as it shimmers and snakes from Alderley, full of life even past dusk when fishermen catch silvery elvers by lamplight, until it spills, churned and spent and muddy, into the Severn Estuary at Chepstow.

The school building is basic: stone built with high windows and a thatch roof, which looks attractive but Mama says is entirely impractical and expensive to maintain. It's so small that children of all ages have to be taught in one room, and the one outside toilet is little more than a wooden plank balanced over a stinky pit. And it's always, *always* cold. In the winter we're allowed to wear fingerless mittens and to bring a blanket from home to keep out the icy, jagged fingers of Jack Frost.

It's half past twelve now; some of the children have gone home, and some sit with me in the school yard, cross-legged on the ground, munching on bread and butter before letting off steam in a game of tag or football, skipping or hopscotch.

I brush my hands on my pinafore, leaving a smudge of chalk; a dull headache moans at my temples. It's been a long morning – Mama has confiscated three catapults already, not to mention several bags of conkers and, more unusually, one white mouse. The little creature sits, affronted, at the front of the class in a square glass container normally reserved for tadpoles. A blue-and-white chequered picnic blanket anchored with several books prevents his escape.

The children are not alone in their fidgetiness – my own uneasiness aside, something hasn't been right at home since Mr Bletchley called last week. Everything feels *off*, like a tilted painting waiting to be tipped back into position. Mama has been unnaturally quiet, and Pa, measured and calm as he usually is, has taken to slamming doors and thumping tables as if shaken up like a snow globe, which only adds to Mama's silent distress.

Bridie and Bertie Fisher run past at breakneck speed. 'Wannaplaytagmiss?' Bertie hollers, not waiting for my response as he hurtles by, red-faced, dimpled and grinning. I shouldn't have favourites, Mama says, but I can't help it. There's something about Bertie Fisher that makes me want to squeeze him tight. He's bursting with joy, a child that brings brightness when he comes into a room, as if an extra lamp has been lit. It's from Bertie's desk that the mouse was liberated, along with a catapult and a mound of tiny brown pellets for ammunition. Mouse poo if you please! Boys are so disgusting.

Bertie looks over his shoulder, yelling, 'Come on, Bridie! We'll play mining. I'm going to find the biggest coal seam in the *worrrrrld* and make our fortune!' He is obsessed with the mine, the silly boy.

On cue, a distant whistle blows twice, the noise floating across the valley from mine to playground. The coalpit is further down the valley, nestled among the trees behind the horseshoe bend in the river, about a twenty-minute walk from the water's edge.

The boys pause their play to listen, distracted by the call of the mine. It will keep calling them until the day they put down their pens, collect their picks and follow their fathers down into the black.

The poor, doomed beggars.

I pull my cardigan tight across my chest, crossing my arms to fend off a sudden chill.

I don't go near the mine if I can help it. There is too much there for me to feel. I don't know if it's my gift or if it's just me, but the weight of sadness from what happened there is so great that it pushes down on me like a heavy dark cloud.

A small brass plaque bears the names of those that perished, six souls lost under tonnes of fallen rubble, six fathers missing from the dinner table. The plaque doesn't mention the endless torture in the minds of the men that witnessed the accident. They see it over and over and over again, each time wondering if they could have done more – helped more – saved someone. What would that do to you, over time?

My father was one of those rescued, having gone down to help with carts and tracks – doing them a favour, an extra pair of hands. When the seam collapsed, he was up top and safe, but the cage slipped and stuck in the shaft, jammed tight on to a ledge, so Pa went to shift it, swinging his legs through the safety hatch at the top and jumping in. The pain in his leg was immediate. The dynamite detonator, a block of solid and immobile metal, was invisible under a pile of black scree, and Pa landed heavily on it, snapping bones and ripping flesh. He managed to free the cage from the ledge before he blacked out. They took his leg to save him.

I look over at Bertie, halo of blond hair and smile as bright and joyful as the sun, and imagine him down there, a child of the eternal night, his lungs full of coal dust, eyes crying black tears, and I truly think my heart may break.

'Did it really only take a week, Peggy?' asks a tiny, birdlike boy with bow legs and large, sorrowful eyes. We don't see George every day. In fact, weeks go by when we don't see him at all, until Mama pays a visit to his family to impress the need for him to be in school.

George Hubbard is Sally's little brother, and on the days he isn't at school he is shoved up a chimney, breathing in black dust as he loosens caulk and checks for nesting birds and wheedles out brushes when they get stuck, earning a pittance for his hard work. It's supposed to be against the law these days, sending up a boy as young as George, but so many people turn a blind eye it's a wonder they don't all bump into each other while they're ignoring all the bad things that go on.

The Hubbards live in two rooms, sleeping where warmest and eating whatever they can get: flour soup with blobs of lard or meat in the form of sparrows, squirrels or pigeons on days when Mr Hubbard is not too drunk to lay traps. He worked down the mine until the accident. After that, the drink became more important to him and the fall into poverty was faster than a stone into a well.

Sally, of course, is working at Clifton Lodge. It doesn't sound so bad, although the hours are long and the work is hard and hand-reddening. I look down at my own, still white and smooth, and hide them beneath my apron. I posted the letter I'd written to Sal on the way to school and asked George if he had heard from her; he had not and said his mother was upset that she rarely hears from her only daughter now she's working at the big house. Mama called in to see the Hubbards just yesterday after school, and when I asked her how it had gone she gave me one of her 'everything is fine' looks, which made my heart twist with worry.

'Sorry, George,' I say, bringing my attention back to him. 'Did what only take a week?'

'The Creation. Did it really only take a week?'

I consider how to respond. Questions like this can be too tempting for me; Mama says it's a skill to temper what you wish to say with what other folk can cope with hearing.

'You know, miss, when God made the world and the animals and the people, like it says in the scriptures.'

'I know what the Creation is, George,' I say, crouching down next to him. 'It's all over the blackboard, for one thing.' Mama must be trying to bore them into silence with her choice of handwriting practice today. 'Seven days doesn't sound particularly long, for all the work that had to be done, does it? Imagine making everything and everyone in seven days! That sounds like –'

'Magic?' suggests George, wide-eyed.

'Like a fairy tale?' says Bertie from the row behind.

I close my eyes and sink into my heels. 'Well . . .'

'So, not really true,' says Bertie definitely.

'*Not true?*' George shouts. 'What? The Bible is a lie?'

'No, no, of course not!' I say. What was I thinking? There are eyes on me, George's chatter having caused a ripple of interest. 'I was wrong to say that, George. I'm sorry. Of course it's true – it's all true.'

'Were you making it up for fun, Peggy?' he asks, looking hopeful. The whites of his wide eyes are tinged with yellow.

'Yes, I'm sorry, I was being too clever for my own good. Forgive me, George.'

'Yes, miss, of course. It's jus' the Bible says, "Blessed are the meek," and Mother says we are meek and that Heaven will be far kinder to us and everything'll be all right when we go up to Heaven. An' if that *isn't* true, then . . .' He sniffs, wiping his nose on the back of his fraying sleeve.

I am such an idiot. 'There's no need to worry, George. Of course it's all true. I'm sorry if I made you doubt it.'

George smiles and I relax, allowing myself a beat of pride at successfully managing such an awkward moment.

'You could ask a whisperling, Miss Peggy,' mumbles Bertie.

My stomach knots. 'Wh-what?'

'Ask a whisperling. About the God stuff. Get it from the horse's mouth, like.' He hastily crosses himself and looks upwards. 'Sorry, God, I didn't mean you're a horse. Rest in peace. Amen.'

My head whooshes and it's like I'm looking down at myself from the ceiling. 'I . . . I'm not sure whisperlings can do that.'

'Can't they, miss? Why not?' Bertie asks.

Why not indeed? In truth, I've never thought to ask. My neck knots in irritation. If I could get my hands on it, there *is* something that could help me with all these questions – the Book of Devona. It's more of a journal really, a collection of personal accounts passed down through the generations like an heirloom, but far more valuable than a string of pearls or a pocket watch. Each Devona woman adds her story to it, passing on her knowledge to those that come after. Pa keeps it under lock and key, says I'm too young and I must wait until I'm older. Pa says it's to protect me. *Pfft.* Pa is wrong, so wrong! It's lonely being the only whisperling I know. I *need* to read that book; there is so much I don't understand.

I'd never say it to him, but it would be so much easier if Mama were the Devona and not him. All Pa wants is to keep me safe, which is fine and noble, but I think Mama understands that being safe isn't about being sheltered from the truth. 'Knowledge is power, Peggy', she says, I'm sure as much for Pa's benefit as mine, and her eyes will slide over to where he usually sits. But she won't go against him, especially not now. Drives me bananas, it does.

'Well, Bertie, I don't know . . . I mean to say, from what I've heard, that isn't something that generally comes up. Perhaps there are rules about it.'

Bertie doesn't answer. His eyes are fixed somewhere over my left shoulder. Too late, I realize we have a visitor.

'You think God would talk to a *whisperling*?' scoffs the Reverend Silas Tate.

The reason for today's blackboard of scriptures is now alarmingly clear.

'Of course! It had to be *you*, Miss Devona, babbling such profanity.' He fixes me with an icy glare. 'The Bible is the only truth, young lady. It's a shame that age has not brought an end to your childish lies and fantasies. You must be careful.' He jabs a hook-like finger at my face, half-moon glasses perched on the end of his beaky nose. 'You wouldn't wish to be thought of as a handmaid to the Devil, would you?'

'I-I'd rather be no one's handmaid, truth be told.' I wipe a speck of his spittle from my neck. 'And Charles Darwin would agree with me about the Creation at least,' I whisper to the floor, unable to stop myself.

His weasel features contort into confused fury, like a cat chasing the reflection of the sun. 'I don't know what game you think you're playing this time, child –'

'Mr Tate, what a lovely surprise,' interrupts my mother. She walks over and extends a hand, which the vicar shakes briefly. A woman in my mother's position should curtsey, or at least dip her head. My mother does neither and I love her for it.

'Is this what you're teaching these children, Mrs Devona? Blasphemy? I obviously need to keep a closer eye on things. An inadequate education is a terrible burden on a child,' he says, glancing at me.

What a stinking hypocrite. It's fine for him, keeping children out of school to make his bed and fix his supper and empty his chamber pot. Sally worked at the vicarage for a short while before getting her position at Clifton Lodge. She hated it – said the vicar was 'a fussy, mean master', and one of the housemaids had been spiteful and sharp-tongued with her too. She'd been glad to leave, even though it meant moving further away from the village.

'Surely it's important for children to learn to think for themselves?' says Mama. 'It can only be a good thing for the future, wouldn't you agree – you being a progressive man, Mr Tate?'

'Of course, yes,' says the vicar. 'However, the scriptures are to be respected, and I'm afraid if I were to report that they are being belittled in a place that relies *so* heavily on donations from the Church . . .' His voice trails away as he apparently feels no need to finish his threat.

'We all rely heavily on the goodness of the Church, Vicar.' Mama's voice is icy. 'Your congregation has dwindled of late and I wonder what will become of your beautiful vicarage? I imagine it takes a pretty penny to maintain.'

Rage boils up from his boots and cooks his face red. Mama has struck a nerve. 'There are limits, madam, even for a progressive man such as myself, and disrespecting God's word requires punishment.' He licks the corner of his mouth where the spittle has congealed to a white blob. 'A little solitude and time for self-reflection is called for, perhaps?'

'No, I really don't see that's necessary,' says my mother, her face white. I grip on to the back of George's chair to steady myself.

'I'm afraid, Mrs Devona, as governor of this school and spokesperson of God in this parish,' he snarls, 'I insist.'

He lunges, grabbing for George, his cassock billowing as he strides towards the front of the class with the tiny wailing boy under his arm.

'It weren't him! It were me!' shouts Bertie, clattering his chair over as he jumps to his feet, but Mr Tate ignores him. The coward. He knows full well that Bertie would put up more of a fight.

'No!' says Mama.

'Now, there's no need for hysterics, dear lady!' he says, kneeling on the floor as if to pray and pulling on a small, round brass handle. It lifts a hatch that opens on to a tight, damp cellar, likely to have been used in olden times to store coal or logs. These days, it contains the odd chair, writing slates, ink and pens. It is freezing cold and quiet enough to hear the hiss of an underground stream that runs inches from its walls. A child can just about stand upright and, if the hatch is shut, they can see nothing at all, so complete is the blackout. 'Down you go, boy!'

There is a wet patch on George's trousers. I step forward. 'No. I'll do it. It was my fault, not George's. I'll go.'

'What's this? A noble sacrifice by Miss Devona?' says Mr Tate.

'Peggy, no,' says Mama. 'Mr Tate, is this really necessary?'

'You would prefer the entire class to be punished, madam?'

'I'll do it, Mama – it's fine,' I say.

The vicar deposits George on the floor, where he curls up like a hedgehog into a ball.

'Very well, Miss Devona,' says Mr Tate. A self-satisfied smile skirts his mouth and, in that moment, I know that this is what he wanted all along. I don't know why, but he wants me out of the way, I'm sure of it. Shoving me into this hole is just the start.

There are five rungs on the ladder to the bottom of the pit and by the time I reach the fourth the hatch is closed and pushing down on my head. My last view of the world was the vicar's eyes peering over his glasses, a smug ghost of a smile playing on his lips. I hate him. I shouldn't, and it's a bad thing to feel, but I don't care. How on earth can that monster claim to be God's messenger?

It's darker down here than the inside of a coffin. There's no light, no air; there's nothing beyond these walls but earth and water. I hear the *fizzshh* of the underground spring. The children say the cellar is haunted, which is nonsense, but all the same . . .

A noise.

There was definitely a noise. Already crouching in this tiny space, I scrunch down still further, close my eyes and stick my fingers in my ears to block it out, whatever it is . . . *Oh! There it is again!* No, not a noise. A voice.

Peggy.

The temperature drops. My scalp tingles.

Together.

Oof! My breath is whipped away. I force open my eyes, squinting as lights and shapes flicker in front of me like images in a zoetrope. The thing judders and flashes so quickly that I strain to make sense of what I'm seeing . . .

It's a girl.

Fear knots in my chest. She is almost transparent, at times no more tangible than my frosty breath. Dust motes, disturbed cobwebs and dirt converge and layer over her as she jerks towards me, hair splaying, haloing around her as if in water. I tunnel into myself. A scream locks in my throat as I stumble in panic and – *Ouch, my head* . . . and then nothing.

She looked like me, I think.

I press the heel of my hand against my temple to quell its throbbing, wincing as I touch a farthing-sized bump already proud on my forehead. I attempt to stand, levering myself up against what I presume to be the thing upon which I hit my noggin: a chair, I think, placed against the wall.

She looked like me.

I have to get out of here. Heart hammering against my ribs, I bang my shaking hands on the hatch. *Please, someone hear me!* I need to find this dead girl. There must have been an accident close by! We need to help her! Unease prickles my neck. But . . . she was so *different* from all the other souls I've seen. Why was that? Spirits on their burn are generally as ordinary in appearance as you or me.

Her juddery movements, the flickering lights, her odd clothing – a shapeless black tunic and what looked like a man's work boots – none of it makes any sense.

And why did she look like *me*?

I have to get out. I pummel again at the hatch, drawing blood from my knuckles. Finally it creaks and opens, flooding the pit with light and air.

'Oh, Peggy, your head!' Mama says, grabbing my arm to help me up the ladder.

'Where is she?'

'Where's who? What do you mean? Did you fall or faint? I'm so sorry, Peg.' Mama puts her arm round me.

I strain my neck to look past her. 'The girl,' I say. 'Where is she?'

My mother stills and puts her hands on my shoulders. She tips her head. 'There is no girl here, Peggy,' she says carefully. 'You've had a shock and a nasty bump to the head. No wonder you're a little confused.'

I nod. Confused is exactly what I am. 'What about Mr Tate? Where is he?'

'Gone,' says Mama haltingly. 'There was . . . an incident.'

'I wanted to scare him,' says Bertie, a red welt flaming on his cheek. 'He was mean.' He sits cross-legged on the floor, next to George, in front of the blackboard. They are sharing the blanket: blue-and-white chequered, used for picnics in the summer, knee-warming in the winter, and today for preventing the escape of a little white mouse.

I look from Bertie to the blanket, to the now empty glass container and understand.

'Oh, Bertie,' I say, as the little boy dissolves into hot, fierce tears.

Mama is stony-faced. I follow her gaze in the direction of the cloakroom. On the floor is a patch of red and white: blood and fur. The mouse. Only its long tail is unmarked. It looks like a string tethering a balloon – a balloon crushed by the stamp of a wrathful man's boot.

A week later and my nerves have settled, although I am unable to shake the cloud of worry that sits heavy on my back. The Reverend Silas Tate has not returned, neither has my raven-haired spectral visitor. For both, I'm grateful. That girl . . . who is she? Why did she appear like that? Why did she *look* like . . . like that? Like me? And what of her message, if that's what it was? 'Together,' she said. Together with whom? I wish I understood.

As if these troubles were not enough, my letter to Sally is, as yet, still unanswered, which dips me further into gloom. Mama is discreetly taking food parcels to the Hubbards' tiny cottage every couple of days; I overheard her tell Pa that Sally's dad was going doolally, not having had any money from the girl in over a fortnight.

It is Saturday, and we are having our weekly outing to Winnie's Tea Room, a popular little cafe in the shadows of the ruins of Alderley Abbey, a twenty-minute cart ride from our cottage. Since Mr Bletchley's visit, the atmosphere at home has been a little frosty and I've yet to fathom why; I'm hoping that today's outing will bring about a thaw and all our moods will lift.

'Good posset, ain't it?' I say, spooning velvety, lemon-flavoured cream into my mouth. 'Posset' is one of those words that sound rude but isn't, and I know it's stupid and childish but it makes us laugh. Usually.

Mama smiles, but it's an effort.

Pa slides his gaze, previously fixed on the white china sugar bowl in the centre of the table, to my face. There's a barely perceptible twitch at the corner of his mouth, and the relief sweeps over me like warm custard over pudding.

'Why, yes, Peg, it is indeed a perfectly pleasant posset. I trust you are finding it sufficiently . . . wibbly?'

I smile at Pa's silliness, but Mama is quiet, still. 'Is everything all right, Mama?' I say carefully.

Mama sighs. 'There's nothing wrong as such, Pegs,' and I know from her use of my nickname that there definitely is. 'You probably know that Mr Bletchley is after us to have another . . . to use us for . . .'

I know what she is trying to say, and also why she's finding it so difficult. It's a perfect autumn afternoon. Although low, the sun is bright and warming, especially as it streams through the gleaming windows of the tea shop. The cafe is fresh and welcoming. There are ribbon-tied posies on white linen tablecloths, snowy bone china, sugar cubes and tiny tongs, starched napkins, and cake forks with polished ivory handles – it's like taking tea on a wedding cake.

So talking about what we must talk about is like emptying a chamber pot on to fresh bedding.

'I know, Mama', I say. 'I thought we would have no more bodies from the gaol after what happened last time . . .' I swallow, and a cloud passes in front of the sun. 'So why has he asked us to take another one?'

Silence weighs heavy. Pa fiddles with the sugar cubes, looking to balance one on top of the other, but the tongs are too tiny for his hands. They drop with a clatter. My mother looks sharply to where my father sits, then back to me.

'It's a child,' says Mama quietly.

'A child? I don't understand.'

The sun slides behind the ruins of the abbey, tipping it into shadow. It looms dark and malevolent, its jagged turrets threatening to pierce the reddening sky. Icy prickles trace a path from my neck and down past my shoulder blades, slicing my spine. A *child*?

'That's why he came to us, Peggy. Because he knows we'd take care of them,' says my father, good to the core.

'I couldn't say no,' adds Mama, kind and strong and decent.

What a position to put my mother and father in! If Bletchley were here right now I'm not sure I wouldn't thump him, uncle or no.

'How old?' I manage.

'I'm not sure,' replies Mama. 'Not yet sixteen though, Pegs.'

They've hanged a child, not a handful of years older than me. How could they? Oh fiddlesticks, I wish Sally were here to talk about this!

*

'What on earth are they supposed to have done?' asks Dora Sweeting, later that evening.

'I've no idea.' I pull my cardigan tighter, so it crosses at the front, and tuck my hands under my armpits. It's cooler sitting here on the landing than in the rest of the house, me on the top step, Dora on the small rocking chair to the left of the staircase.

'It would have to have been something pretty terrible, for thems to make 'em swing,' she says, pulling a face. 'Could a kiddie commit such a crime?'

I shrug. 'I don't know, Dora, I really don't. Should it matter – their age – though, if they've done something truly awful?'

What we don't say is that the child must have murdered someone. It's the most likely crime to warrant such punishment, but it seems too ugly a thought. So we sit there awhile in silence, Dora and me.

'You need to look after 'em,' says Dora finally.

'I agree,' I say. Because if not us, then who? Whatever this child did, however awful, they need care and compassion on this part of their journey. I don't allow myself to think of what will happen afterwards, when those that call themselves scientists take their turn. I swallow the bile that's risen in my throat.

'I should probably be off now,' says Dora. 'Don't forget to tell him, will you?'

I smile and wave a piece of paper at her. 'I've got it all written down, I promise. Thank you for dropping by.'

'You're a good girl, Peggy love. Maybe I'll see you again sometime.'

'I'd like that,' I say, but I know it isn't likely. Not for a good long while anyway. A soft shimmer, a candlelight halo, blurs the edges of Dora's slight frame and slowly, slowly, layer by shimmering cobweb layer, the light builds until she is golden and glorious and full of love and light. Her gaze is somewhere above my head and, when she glances back at me and smiles, my heart swells partly with a touch of sadness, but far more with an overwhelming joy. And then she is gone.

I stand, stretch and walk downstairs to the dressing room, where Dora Sweeting's body has been resting since her family brought her in that morning. Dora had been ill for some time, her once bright mind slowly closing down. I stroke her cheek with the back of my hand and her skin is papery and cool, her expression rested and peaceful. 'Goodnight, Dora,' I whisper. 'That was a most beautiful burn.'

I am in that strange hollow between wake and sleep. The oily scent of the lamp, freshly doused, drifts through the room and something catches my mind on the end of its line, tugging me towards it.

'Dora?' I say, knowing it isn't her. I still have the unsettled feeling that's been with me since Sally was last here, when I felt something, some energy, snap and then fade. Except . . . it didn't fade. Not completely.

I sit up, uneasy. The moon casts looming shadows over the whitewashed walls, the rough plaster lending depth and form; a doll becomes a monster, a pencil pot turns into jagged teeth, a chair transforms into a hangman's gallows. A breath catches in my chest and I hold it until the tremble passes. What is happening? Why am I so jittery? Throwing off the covers, I walk to the nightstand and splash my face, grateful for the surety of cold water on my skin. It's my imagination, that's all. My parents are on edge and it's playing on my mind, what with that and Mr Tate and – *What was that?* Something . . . something *static* . . . crackles in the air.

Oh!

Everything sparkles and shudders like a kaleidoscope hit by lightning, and there in the middle of the room – her black tunic slipping off one shoulder, her long dark hair (*just like mine!*) tumbling over her other shoulder – is the girl. She sputters towards me and her mouth widens in a silent scream . . . and I turn and I run, skittering across the landing, down the stairs and into the kitchen. There, in front of the stove, I huddle beneath Wolf's blanket, sharing her warmth. Only when a watery autumn sun starts leaching through the kitchen curtain do I dare return to my room, with Wolf for company. I peek round my bedroom door. The girl, whoever she was, has gone. Everything is as it was.

I wish I could say the same about me.

Head throbbing, I rewrite the note from Dora to make it legible and head out into the early-morning light before the rest of the house greets the day.

Dora's son is Mr Sweeting, the baker, so this must be done even earlier than usual, given that he fires up his bread ovens not long after daybreak. Wolf barely lifts a sleepy eyelid as I sneak out of the scullery door, through the garden gate and on to the back lane, yawning as I go.

Sometimes, if a message from a spirit to their loved one isn't too specific, there's no need for a note and I can get away with making a passing comment. Admittedly, it isn't always easy to shoehorn words from the dead into a conversation, especially if I don't know the person very well. 'I'm sure he always loved you' or 'She would want you to be happy' are all well and good, but something like 'It's always best to check under the coal scuttle for lost dentures, don't you think?' is more of a bother, let me tell you. If the villagers don't suspect me of being a whisperling, then at the very least they must think me a bit odd.

It's bright but nippy this morning: not quite a frost but there's a definite crunch underfoot. It's a beautiful time of year, the colours of the forest warming from greens to burnished orange, soon to be aflame with golds and reds. I walk the path from home down to the village in record time; without my overcoat I'm far too cold to dawdle. I can picture my coat hanging in the cupboard under the stairs, but the door creaks and would have given me away if I'd tried to fetch it. I'm sure Mama wouldn't have stopped me, but sometimes it's easier to beg forgiveness than ask permission, so why take the risk?

I love this time of day when few have risen. The river is in view, inky black, dusted with mist and perfectly still. The village too is quiet, the general store, butcher's and greengrocer's still to throw up their shutters. The Miners Arms, with its low, whitewashed walls, marks the end of the village, and there are plenty of villagers who have never ventured further than that, nor have any desire to do so.

It's easy to slip the note under the door of the bakery and I walk back in a more relaxed fashion, stopping to look at the birds still asleep at the edge of the river, beaks tucked under wings, the tangled reeds and mudflats making a perfect mattress.

I see her then, under the water, her dark hair splayed and spread into the black mire, her face twisting as she rises and reaches for me, all the while flickering and flashing like a quivering flame. Terror rips through me, and I scream. I turn and run and run and –

'*Oof!*'

I thud into a sturdy, tweed-covered torso.

'Young lady, are you quite well? . . . Peggy? What on earth are you doing out here at this hour?'

'Ambrose! What are *you* doing out here at this hour?' Not that it matters. My shoulders relax. I'm safe. I'm –

'Hey! You! You been stickin' notes through my door? Is this from you?'

'Hello, Mr Sweeting,' I say. He's wearing his trousers but no shirt, braces pulled up over a long-sleeved vest, and on his feet his hobnail boots. In his haste, he clearly hasn't given his outfit much thought.

'Was this you?' he says, shaking the piece of paper at me, so close it fans my face. I take a step back. 'I knew you were one of them creepers – everybody says so!'

'I say, Mr Sweeting, there's no need for that,' says Ambrose, placing himself between us like a barrier. 'I'm sure you're mistaken about Miss Devona, and, besides, we don't use that terminology any more.' He turns to me, amused. 'Did you write the note, Peggy?'

'Well, did you?' asks Mr Sweeting, less aggressively this time. His eyes are rimmed red. 'Sorry for getting so agitated. It was just a bit of a shock, like. I don't care if you're a creep– if you're a, er, whisperling or the Queen of Sheba. Doesn't make any odds to me. I've got a poster and everything. Live and let live, I say. But the note . . . was it you?'

I think of Pa telling me to keep my trap shut, and say nothing.

'May I, Mr Sweeting?' requests Ambrose.

'No!' I say, Pa's advice falling out of my head. 'It's none of your boggin' business, Ambrose Shipwell!'

'Peg– Miss Devona, please!' Ambrose holds out his gloved hand and Mr Sweeting passes him the note. I grab at it, but Ambrose raises his hand into the air, out of my reach, and takes a step away.

He gazes at the note for an age before speaking.

'What? Need help with the long words, Mr *Chimp*well?' I say stubbornly.

Ambrose glares at me, and I feel something like guilt when I see his eyes are watery. He reads the note aloud and I stare at the ground. '*Dora (Mum) would like you to know that the answers to your questions are: yes, I am; yes, you definitely are; no, not for all the tea in China. Sincere condolences for your loss. Signed, A Friend.*' He pauses. 'Does it mean anything to you, Mr Sweeting?'

The baker pauses and rubs his eyes with the heel of his hand. 'Dora – Mum, I mean – at the end, she didn't know who I was or where she was, but we cared for her as best we could, like. Every night, when I went to see 'er before we turned in, I'd ask 'er three things.' He looks up, cheeks wet with tears, and I glance away, ashamed that I caused this.

'What things?' asks Ambrose, biting down hard on his bottom lip.

'Firstly, I'd ask her if she was still in there somewhere. So she was, then, wasn't she? I knew she was.' He pauses, gets himself together before carrying on. 'Secondly, I asks . . . ask*ed* her if I was a decent son, if I was doin' all right by 'er. I definitely am, she says. Well, isn't that somethin'? An' thirdly, I'd ask her whether she'd have liked to have had a different life. To 'ave been more than the mother of a local baker.' His voice cracks and a hot tear rolls unchecked down my chilled cheek. '"Not for all the tea in China," she says, eh?' He looks at me, and smiles. 'Thank you, Peggy.'

Ambrose accompanies me home, which is annoying. He is far too interested in the note I left for Mr Sweeting, even though I haven't admitted that I'm the one who wrote it.

'I think you were trying to be kind,' he says, 'offering comfort to those that have lost a loved one. I commend you.'

'Oh, hark at you! You "commend" me, do you?'

'Of course! Being a whisperling is a skill to be revered and cherished. You shouldn't have to hide away,' he says, gloved hand twirling the end of an undetectable moustache.

'Good goblins, Ambrose, you're about five minutes older than me, so stop talking like that –

you sound just like Mr Bletchley. And stop twiddling your face. There are but three hairs on it!'

Ambrose sniffs theatrically, draws a lacy handkerchief from his sleeve and dabs at his bone-dry eyes. 'You wound me, Peggy. Although I'm sure you'd be an excellent addition to the Psychic Emporium, I think you're a horror and it would be dreadful to have you around annoying me day after day.'

'You . . . want me to come to Bristol?' I ask, surprised.

'Of course not. You're awful.' (I try not to smile at this.) 'I have many, many friends,' he continues, 'and you would be entirely in the way. But, in spite of the *huge* personal inconvenience to me, I think it would be good for you.'

'Good for me? What, working at the emporium – conning people, you mean? Mediums are a joke, a parlour game for posh women bored of doing their cross-stitch. People can't talk to the dead, not like that, not on demand. It's nonsense.'

'How do you know for sure, Peggy? You seem to think you're the only one, but you're not. Those posters can't only be about you. There must be others, so why not these other women too?' For once, I don't know how to answer.

Ambrose stops walking and turns to me. 'I know you don't want to confide in me, Peggy, and that's fine. But why not try it? You could earn a little bit for the family while you do so.'

'How much?' I say, too quickly. We're no worse off than anyone else, but I know how hard my parents work for the little they get – as a schoolmistress my mother earns a pittance, and carpenters, even a master craftsman like Pa, don't exactly make a fortune.

'Oh, about a guinea per sitting,' he says casually.

'A *guinea*?' I yelp. That's more than Mama earns in a month, and about what Pa would have got for a bench that took him a week to make.

'You see?' cajoles Ambrose. 'You may even enjoy yourself. And Mr Bletchley thinks it would do you good to get out of the village for a while.'

I stamp my foot. 'Oh, Mr Bletchley, Mr Bletchley! Mr Bletchley knows *nothing*! Yes, he's my *uncle*, but it's just a word, it's meaningless – he knows nothing about me! Nothing!'

Ambrose steps back and fiddles with the lace frill of his shirt. 'You must admit, though, it's a bit of a coincidence for a man to run a psychic emporium when there are rumours of his niece being –' he buries his face in his collar – 'psychic,' he mutters.

Truly, there are days I could kill Jedediah Bletchley, and this is one of them. He has made things so much more difficult for me and my family by operating in the open. *Why* open the Psychic Emporium, *why* invest in an undertaker's, and why, why, *why* employ Ambrose Shipwell, of all people? Someone who has known your secret-whisperling niece since forever? I pull up my skirts and stomp towards home, boots clacking so hard on the cobbles that they spark.

Ambrose yells at me to wait but I ignore him, fury fuelling me like an angry steam train. He puts on a burst and eventually draws level, grabbing my arm as he puffs and huffs.

'Wait!' He leans and puts his hands on his knees to get his breath back. '*Foof*, that's quite a slope. I'm sorry. I'll stop asking, I promise. It's just with the posters around the village and everything . . . I don't know, perhaps it would do you good to be in a more cosmopolitan environment.'

'Alderley is perfectly *cosmopolitan* enough, thank you,' I say defensively.

'Is it? Mr Sweeting is possibly one of the more liberal fellows in the village and even he was unsettled by coming face to face with you, a whisperling. People can put up posters, mind their language and imagine they're as accepting as the next person . . . but when it's on their own doorstep? I'm not so sure . . . All it takes is a few failed crops, Peggy, and they'll be looking for someone to blame, and I don't need to remind you what happened to the witches.'

'And you think that the city, where they hang children for doing goodness-knows-what, is a safer place for me to be?' The words catch and I bring a hand to my neck, rubbing at the soft skin of my throat.

Ambrose scuffs at the floor with the toe of his boot. 'Oh. You know about that, do you?'

'Mama told me.' I pause. 'Ambrose, why exactly are you lurking around the village so early this morning?'

'Mr Bletchley is at your folks' house. Something to discuss. Wanted me to get him a newspaper. I told him the shop wouldn't be open yet but he insisted. I was right, of course – it won't open for another hour or so.'

'He wanted you out of the way, in other words.'

'No, I'm sure that's not it. I'm his assistant.'

'Yes, Ambrose. He wanted you out of the way!' I grab his hand and drag him up the hill. 'Come on, let's go and find out why.'

We are both out of breath when we get to my gate. Pa is in the garden with a birch twig broom, perhaps about to sweep the chicken coop, whistling tunelessly. I have a flash of a sweet memory – Mama and Pa twirling about the kitchen, Mama shrieking with laughter with floured hands above her head as Pa lifts and whirls her around like a spinning top. The way he looked at her then is the way he still looks at her nowadays. I try not to look at the space where his leg once was, his trouser leg folded up and pinned above the knee. Sadness punches me in the gut.

'Is Mr Bletchley still here? What did he want?' I ask. My father stops whistling, and just then my mother comes out into the yard, followed by Mr Bletchley.

'I don't know. I've been out here,' says Pa, adjusting his braces. They are his good braces, the red ones with the navy piping. Mama would definitely have something to say about that.

'Good day, Peggy,' says Mr Bletchley, tipping his hat. 'Ah, no luck with the newspaper, Ambrose, my boy?' He tucks a thumb under the velvet lapel of his frock coat. With that and his fancy waistcoat, stiff shirt and cravat, he's as trussed up as a turkey and I'll wager he's never done a day's labour in his entire life. 'Right,' he announces, 'I'll be off to pay my respects to the Hubbards, then back to the city in time for breakfast!'

My heart lifts. 'The Hubbards? Have you had word of Sally? I wrote to her but she –'

'No, no, nothing like that . . . no.' He turns to Ambrose. 'Well, lad, I'm certain that shop will be open to sell you my newspaper now, so off you go.'

'But . . .' Ambrose doesn't sound too pleased. I throw him a look and he scowls back at me.

'Well?' demands Mr Bletchley. 'What are you waiting for, lad? I'll meet you back at the carriage in an hour.' As Ambrose starts walking back down the hill, Bletchley turns to my parents. 'Good day to you, Lydia. We'll talk again.' My father bristles at the familiarity, but says nothing.

We stand in silence until Mr Bletchley is well out of earshot.

'I thought you were going to put a note under the door and get out of there, Peg,' says Pa. 'Best put the kettle on, I suppose.' With that, we go back into the house.

'So, this ghost girl you keep seeing,' says Pa, 'do you recognize her?'

I hadn't meant to tell him about her, but I had little choice. I need his advice. Spirits don't scare me, save for the odd one or two, and thankfully those are few and far between. Besides, there are *rules*. Rules that this juddering apparition seems not to stick to. For starters, how is she following me around? Spirits are usually attached to places, not people. Perhaps during their burn a spirit may reach out to a loved one – or to a whisperling like me if they want to and are close by – but, other than that, it isn't possible.

That's why Mr Bletchley's Psychic Emporium is so preposterous. Even if his psychics are genuine, which I very much doubt, no spirit worth its salt would be hanging around just *waiting* to be summoned to a terraced house in the middle of Bristol, in order to put on a performance for a guinea a throw. Or would they? I sink on to the table, resting my forehead on the knotty surface. What do I know?

'No, I don't recognize her,' I mumble into the wood. Sighing, I sit up and take a sip of tea, scalding my tongue in the process. 'At least, I don't think so.'

'And she's appeared in your bedroom, at school . . .'

'Yes. And now by the river.'

'But there are rules . . .' Pa says, trailing off.

'I *know*!'

Pa smiles at me. He knows all about the rules, being the one who told me about them.

'I know,' I repeat more quietly. 'That's why I don't understand how she keeps appearing.' This girl is proving to be a very different sort of ghost. I steel myself. 'Perhaps if I could read the Book of Devona for myself . . .?'

'No, not this again, Peg. You're not ready. Perhaps in a year or so, when you're a little older.'

Not this again! I love Pa, but I could scream. It's easy for him to say I'm not ready because it's not him that has to deal with it. Pa is a carrier, meaning that he can protect and advise, but nothing more. It's the women in the Devona bloodline who have the power. Only the women. Not that you would know it.

'Mama thinks I should,' I whisper to the table.

Pa sighs. 'I'm well aware of that, Peggy. Your mother's hardly been backwards about voicing her opinions.' He glances around, as if nervously checking she isn't within earshot. 'But, when all's said and done, I have to do what I think is right. And that is to quietly go about our business without drawing attention, to keep you safe. And part of that is deciding when the time is right for you to read the book. Mama did agree with me, you know, when you were younger.'

'But I'm older now!' I protest. 'And Mama –'

'Your mama isn't a Devona.'

'More's the pity,' I mutter. Pa may know about whisperlings but he's entirely clueless about young girls. Mama would manage my worries far better if she only had all the knowledge at her disposal. *She* knows I'm not a baby any more. But Mama isn't allowed to read the book because she isn't 'Devona by blood'. Oh, these *ridiculous* rules!

I've tried over the years to sneak a glance at the book whenever I thought Pa wasn't watching. It's kept in the parlour, hidden away at the back of the dresser in a locked box lined with velvet. The box was made by Pa after the last time I dared look at the book. Leather-bound and the size of a large

Bible, the creamy pages are now edged with yellow and thickened with damp. Loose leaves and scraps of paper are interspersed between the pages – messages and notes hastily written and hidden by past whisperlings, away from prying eyes.

I've read nothing of it at all in the last few years. I've not even tried, out of a begrudging respect for Pa (and because he has hidden the key), but, from what I can remember, the writing is so faint, and phrased so strangely, it's difficult to understand any of it at first glance. Passages detailing spirits caught in limbo; doors that shouldn't be opened; warnings about forces that are too strong; how spirits, in some form or other, are whirling around us *all the time* – I've pushed all that information to one side, because it shook me so. But surely, now that I'm twelve, it's best for me to know everything there is to know about being a whisperling, good and bad?

Pa taps his chin with a teaspoon, ignoring me, like he always does when I ask about the book. 'I don't think we should tell your mother about this ghost girl – at least, not until we're more certain about what we're dealing with. You can have Wolf in your room until things settle down,' he offers. 'But I'm sorry – I can't help more than that.'

Ignoring the howl of frustration that screams in my belly, I nod, knowing full well I will tell Mama anyway.

I breathe in and out slowly, deliberately, bringing my temper under control. 'Do you think Mr Sweeting will tell anyone else about my note?' I ask. 'What if it gets back to Mr Tate?'

'I don't think he will. Don't worry yourself, Pegs.'

'How can you be sure?'

'I can't, but I truly can't see what Tate would do about it, even if he had proof. Even the law is on your side these days.'

'The vicar was very angry when he was at the school. I've never seen him quite so fire and brimstone before. I don't understand why he hates me so.'

'Honestly?' Pa rubs his face. 'I think you unsettle him, Peg. He's heard the rumours, like everyone has, but he's also seen your gift for himself when you tried to pass him that message about the accident in the mine. You were an innocent little girl; there was no deceit about you. But if he had believed you then, that would make him question everything he knows about the afterlife. He probably never thought he'd meet a whisperling in his lifetime. No doubt he considered whisperlings just part of folklore, like most people.'

'You'd think he'd be pleased, though,' I say. 'He'd have proof that there is some sort of life after death.'

'I'm not sure he sees it like that, Peg. Perhaps he thinks it would damage his standing in the parish if everyone knew about your skill. Or perhaps . . . perhaps he's just plain jealous.' The expression on his face crushes the laugh in my throat.

'Pa?'

'Perhaps I'm being too flippant, telling you not to worry. Our Mr Tate is like a wild animal under attack. He could be dangerous.'

I take this in. And, not for the first time, I wonder what Pa would say if he knew I'd started writing a whisperling journal of my own.

It is Thursday and on his way back from Dora Sweeting's funeral Ambrose pays me a visit.

'You were quite the topic of conversation,' says Ambrose, warming himself in front of the stove. He keeps stepping from one foot to the other, like a cat on a hot stone.

'I doubt that,' I say. 'I suspect you're hearing things – or mishearing; perhaps your hat is somehow muffling your ears.'

Ambrose colours, and removes his bowler which is far too big for him. 'No, I don't think so, Peggy,' he says, smoothing out his hair, which is longer than the fashion and curls at the nape. He looks at the floor, barely making eye contact as I hand him a glass of milk. 'If it's true – what you can do, I mean – then little wonder Jedediah is so keen for you to work for him.'

'Is he still on about that?'

'Not in so many words, but I know that Mr Sweeting's told him about the note.'

'Oh great. Well, there's no point discussing it,' I say. 'And perhaps I should let Mr Jedediah Bletchley know that you refer to him so casually when he's out of earshot. *Jedediah* may sack you and then imagine what your pa would say! He's so pleased you're off in Bristol honing your business skills under *Jedediah's* watchful eye, getting you ready for when you come to take over the family seat. I know all about these things, being a rightful heir to one myself – the heir to the grand house of Devona.' I bow in mock ceremony, extending my arms and indicating our tiny kitchen with a flourish.

I expect him to laugh, but he looks downcast. It bothers me that this bothers me so much. Ambrose sips his milk and wipes his mouth with a silk square pulled from his sleeve, like a magician. Nerves ripple from him like a stone thrown into water.

'What's wrong, Ambrose?'

'I have to tell you something, Peggy. I've been skirting around the houses about it, but it's only because I don't know how to say the words.'

'What is it?'

'It's to do with what Mr Bletchley came to see your mother about the other day.'

'About having the body from the gaol? Mama has been wrestling with her conscience about it. I admit it doesn't sit well with me either, but if anyone should look after that poor body, then who better than us? No offence, what with you working at that other undertaking business and all.'

'No, you're quite right. It'll definitely be better for her here. But that wasn't all of it.'

'Wait, did you say "*her*"?' The room swims. First there'd been the shock of learning the body from the gaol was that of a child, and now to learn it's a girl . . . 'I hadn't for one moment considered it would be a girl. Go on.'

Ambrose pales to the white of his pocket square. 'Like I said – that isn't all of it. I don't know how to tell you this, Peggy. I'm so sorry. The body . . . it's Sally.'

'What do you mean, "it's Sally"?' I say, bewildered.

'The girl. The body. It's Sally Hubbard.'

'No!' I cry, sinking to the floor. Ambrose is immediately next to me, hands gripping my shoulders, shushing me. I know not what pitiful sounds I make, only that I wail and wail, unable to keep control. *No!* It can't be true. Sally's no murderer! Sally's my friend, my lovely friend, the sister of little George – oh! *George*, George! What will he do? Sally's ma – her poor, drunken father . . . Do they even know? I'm not sure I can bear to see my friend laid out in a coffin, to see her pass from this life into the next, if she has not moved on there already.

'But what did she do?' I say. 'Why did no one tell me?'

'They say she killed her mistress, Lady Stanton. I only found out myself a couple of days ago. Your ma knew the murderer was someone from the Lodge, but not that it was Sally.'

'Mama *knew*?' This must be Pa's doing. He wants to keep me in the dark about *everything*.

'Don't be mad at your ma, Peggy. She didn't know for certain and it's likely Mr Bletchley told her to keep quiet because things are . . . well, they're complicated. They say Sally killed Lady Stanton in a rage.'

'I mean, yes, Sally's got a temper, but, no, no – she wouldn't! Oh, Ambrose, when will they bring her body here? When is she coming? Surely it'll be soon? I can't have missed the chance to say goodbye! I promised her we'd go to the seaside,' I finish desolately.

'In a couple of weeks, I expect.' He pauses. 'After the trial.'

'*After* the trial . . .? What, you mean she's still alive?' I punch Ambrose's arm. 'Why didn't you say so!'

'Ow! I'm sorry!'

'Where is she? In Bristol Gaol? Can I go there and see her?'

'I don't know, Peggy. I doubt it. They don't usually allow visitors before a trial . . . but I could ask,' he adds, seeing my desperate face.

'Ambrose, if she hasn't had a trial, then why are they arranging who will be laying out her body? How do they know she's guilty?' Blood pounds in my ears as Ambrose helps me to my feet. He pulls out a kitchen chair and I sit heavily.

'You tell me,' says Ambrose. 'I'll not lie; the whole thing seems wrong to me. Even Mr Bletchley is unsettled by it – I'm sure he is. He says he's been told that the evidence against Sally is beyond doubt, but even so . . .'

I look at Ambrose, twisting his enormous hat round and round in his hands as if trying to rub away the rim. 'Why are you telling me this?' I ask.

'There's nothing *I* can do,' he says. 'I wouldn't know how to begin.' He puts his hat down and looks me square in the eye. 'But you do, Peggy. *You* know. Don't you?'

He's right. I do know.

I know I must go to Clifton Lodge to speak with Lady Stanton's spirit before her burn ends. I must find out the truth.

I must save Sally.

'What does your father think? I assume you've asked him,' asks Mama stiffly. She is unhappy with me and has met my enthusiastic plan to go to Bristol with cool disapproval.

The temperature everywhere has dipped. This morning, when I let Wolf out to do her business, a layer of frost cobwebbed the yard. I shiver despite the oppressive warmth of the kitchen. Our meal of hot vegetable soup and thick chunks of bread has not been enough to effect a thaw in the chilly atmosphere that's descended between my mother and me. Pa is at the coal mine; they've been doing some maintenance for a few days, fixing carts and relaying tracks. He can't exactly help down there, but he likes to keep an eye on things. It chills me further, knowing he's there, especially on such a morning.

Mama may be unhappy with me, but I am *furious* with her.

'Of course I've asked him,' I say. 'Pa said it was a fine idea.'

'He did?'

'Well, he said he could understand why I would want to do it and that he'd support me.' (What he actually said was that I should think on it and not make any rash decisions, but he meant the rest too, I'm sure.) I glare at Mama over my soup bowl through the curling steam. 'Ask him yourself if you don't believe me.'

It's like I've slapped her. 'I know you're upset with me, Peggy –'

'You should have told me,' I growl. 'I had to hear it from Ambrose. *You knew.* You knew it was Sally, yet you didn't tell me.'

'No. I didn't know, not straight away. I needed time to consider what could be done, Peggy. I know how impetuous you are, and I couldn't risk you running off to try to save the day all by yourself. It's not safe, especially for a whisperling; besides, you're a *child* and if you think I believe

95

for *one moment* that your father would disagree with that –'

'At least it's better than staying here and doing nothing,' I snap.

'NO!' Mama slams her hand on the table. 'At what point did I say do nothing? Of course we must do something! Just not whatever the first head-in-the-clouds idea you have. So tell me, Peggy – what exactly is your plan?'

'I don't know yet. Maybe –'

'Maybe hightailing it to Bristol on a whim? What next, eh? Falling in with Jedediah at the emporium? Are you sure this is about Sally and not just you running away from your so-called boring, provincial life?'

'Mama! This has nothing to do with Mr Bletchley! Ambrose suggested I could stay there if it was too late to get a carriage home, that's all!' *As if* I'd wish to have anything to do with that traitor! Tears bubble up from my chest; my breath catches in my throat. I picture Sally being led up to the gallows and I think my heart may break. 'All I want to do is ask Lady Stanton what happened!'

'Oh, love, I'm sorry. I know, I know.' Mama covers my hands with her own and grips them tight. 'I didn't mean it. I just don't want to lose you.'

'You're not going to lose me, Mama – why would you even think such a thing?'

'I . . . I . . . don't, of course I don't. But what good will it do, you going there? Even if you speak with Lady Stanton's spirit, which is unlikely as she died nigh on two weeks ago now, who would you tell? Who would believe you? And who knows what trouble it would stir up for you, having anything to do with that ridiculous circus of Jedediah's. We've been so careful . . .'

She's right, of course. By rights, the burn doesn't last that long, at least in most cases. But if Lady Stanton has been wronged – not, I pray, by Sally – then there's a chance she's looking for someone to talk to. I have to try. Mama stands and brushes down her skirts, tells me no, she won't agree to me going to Bristol and I'm not to mention it again. I swallow down my anger, knowing this is not the end of it.

I'll do anything to clear Sally's name. Anything. Even defy Mama.

8

Sunday. There has been no thaw in Mama's resolve and the frostiness between us creeps out into the wider world. Church is so cold that the congregation's shivers could ring the bells by themselves. Two small boys in the pew in front of us puff on rolled-up bits of paper, pretending to smoke. Freezing half to death while listening to an odious man preaching to those that are far more decent than himself is no way to spend the Sabbath, to my mind anyway. I'm almost envious of Pa, who's still overseeing the small team down at the pit getting things ready for the week ahead. How I'll get through Mr Tate's sermon I'll never know. Will the man ever stop droning on? I'm not sure I'll ever get his dirgeful voice out of my head, nor the image of that poor squashed mouse. *All things bright and beautiful?* I don't think so!

I fiddle with my gloves and glance around the congregation. I swear the church hushed when Mama and I walked in. Mr Sweeting said an awkward hello and then buried his head in his prayer book, as did most other folk. I thought I saw Bertie Fisher at the back of the church, but when I looked again he wasn't there. Only Mrs Dulwich the chemist, sitting in her usual spot in the front pew, turned her head to nod at me. I smiled awkwardly back, realizing with a slap that if Sally *had* lobbed a stone through her window that last Saturday morning we spent together, then she'd probably have been fired by Lady Stanton and would be here today, sitting beside me, trying not to laugh in the quiet bits.

Sally's family aren't here, which is no surprise given the state Annie Hubbard, Sally's ma, was in when we looked in first thing. You know when they say someone is broken? I hadn't realized how accurate a description that was until today. With no lamps lit and no answer to our knock, Mama pushed open the Hubbards' scullery door, let out a gasp and ran towards a barely smouldering fire. I couldn't tell at first, so dull and dark was it in the freezing little cottage, that the pile of rags that Mama gathered to her was Annie, crumpled like a discarded marionette, the strings of hope and pride that kept her upright all these years now brutally cut. Mama says Annie Hubbard was always a fine-looking woman, a May Queen back in the day, with hair as red as her daughter's but poker-straight and glossy as spun silk. They were fun once, Sally's folks, given to tomfoolery and quick to laugh. They would give you the shirt off their back, should your need be greater than theirs. I remember playing hoops and hopscotch with Sally in the yard and George senior joining in while Annie rested her hands on her pregnant belly and laughed at her husband's antics. That was before the pit collapse, though. After that, they folded in on themselves – and now this.

Mama re-laid their fire and I tidied up and put away the bread and eggs that we'd brought. I ignored the stench of poteen that sharpened the air and the *tip tip tip* of water dripping into the bucket set beneath the hole in the thatch. We left them then, promising to do what we could to help.

I will not break this promise. I will *not*.

The vicar bores on. 'We must pray for those that have lost their way,' he intones, and I inwardly roll my eyes. 'Who would have thought that in this small community there could lurk such wickedness?'

What?

I sit up sharply. A ripple of discord flutters around the congregation. I lean close to Mama and hiss in her ear, 'He's talking about Sally, isn't he? He's basically saying she's guilty!'

He continues, his oration gaining in fervour and volume. 'This is a time for us to come together to cast out evil, to reject those who would disobey God's laws. The only way for true salvation is to pray together, to look to the Church for guidance, to be guided by the righteous. Those who turn away –' he points accusingly at the congregation, running his finger along every pew until we all shrink back guiltily – 'are all sinners, like that murderous, *ungodly girl*!' He shouts the last two words, slamming his hand on the edge of the pulpit.

A flutter of nervous laughter somewhere in the congregation is quickly covered by coughing. Mama slips a gloved hand into mine and squeezes it hard. 'He's gone quite mad, I fear,' she whispers, and my heart lifts. Perhaps the thaw has begun.

I nod. 'Like a wild animal, backed into a corner.'

She looks at me questioningly.

'Something Pa said,' I reply.

Finally, the service comes to an end and we shuffle out of our pew, giving a hasty sign of the cross towards the altar. At the barn-sized double door we endure a reluctant, clammy handshake with Mr Tate before walking out to freedom.

I see him then, standing outside the churchyard by the lychgate, his hands resting on the low wall. He beckons me over, and so I leave my mother's side and walk down the path towards him.

'Bertie?' I say. 'What are you doing here? Is Bridie with you?'

'I had to see you, miss,' he says. He is shining, scrubbed and neat, his blond hair white in the crisp morning sun. He's wearing his Sunday best and looks ready for church, or a tea party. 'Bridie's at home with Ma.'

'You look very smart, Bertie. I thought I saw you in church.'

He smiles, humouring me. 'You know I wasn't there, miss.'

He's right. I know. His body is as flimsy as warm breath in cold air. I see the gnarls and knots in the wood of the ancient lychgate through his small, insubstantial hands. Grief reaches inside me and crushes my heart. It's a moment before I can speak and, when I do, my voice shakes. 'What happened to you, Bertie?'

'I got in,' he says, 'but then I fell asleep.'

'You did?' I say.

'You needs to tell 'em,' he says, nodding towards the church, 'they needs to get there. I went cos I wanted to help.'

I swallow, a hot, fat tear sliding down my face. 'Get where, Bertie?' I ask, already knowing what his answer will be.

'The pit, miss. They's got to get to the mine. There's water,' he says, and he reaches for me. I feel pressure on my arm and when I look down there's a handprint on the sleeve of my dress. A wet handprint. 'Tell my da I'm sorry.'

Not again. Let this not be happening again. I close my eyes and Bertie's silhouette shines in the darkness. 'I knew you were a whisperling, miss. I'm glad it's you I got to see.' And then a whisper, a breath on the breeze. 'Your pa said to get you. Hurry.'

'Bertie?' I say, but he's already gone. I steady myself against the gate and wipe the back of my hand across my tear-stung face, a howl of grief pushing up from my chest. But there's no time to stand there and mourn – I have to get help. I've got to get help now or I'll be grieving for all of 'em down there, not just my lovely, bright, joyful Bertie. I crush the tears down into my sore heart and run.

There's no time to worry about what they'll think of me. I scramble back towards the church, shouting and screaming until my lungs may burst. 'Accident! There's been an accident down the pit! Please, quickly, we have to go, we have to help!'

'How do you know?' shouts a voice.

'I ... I ... please, I just know. I heard ... something,' I say.

'We should listen to her – she's one of them! A cree– a whisperling!' cries Mr Sweeting. Murmurs bubble through the villagers and I step closer to Mama.

'Calm down, everyone,' says Mr Tate, glaring at me over his glasses. 'There's no need for such an unseemly display, Miss Devona. What on earth are you raving about? There's no one down the pit today. It's a Sunday.'

'But there is,' I cry. 'There's a snagging team down there, fixing rails and carts for next week.

Please, Mr Tate, they'll listen to you. Please, we have to go! There's been a flood. Mama, Mama – we have to go!'

'I believe my daughter,' says Mama. 'We have to get to the pit.' She turns to the unsettled crowd. 'Everyone, we must hasten to the mine. There's been an accident and we'll need all able-bodied men to help. There's rescue equipment on site – let's hurry!'

'With respect, Mrs Devona,' says Mr Tate, his jaw tight with annoyance, 'we all know Margaret is prone to certain . . . flights of fancy, but this is taking it rather too far. Perhaps a spell in the Bristol Lunatic Asylum would do her some good. A place where every so-called whisperling should be, in my opinion.' His eyes burn through my bonnet, into my brain, but I don't care.

'With respect, Mr Tate, you and I both know that sometimes my daughter's . . . *intuition* should be listened to,' says Mama. Then she lowers her voice and leans in to him and almost hisses, 'If this delay causes harm to *one* hair upon *one* head, I swear I'll not rest until you pay, even if I have to take down the Church of England brick by brick to do it.'

A low, slow wail of a siren reaches us from across the valley and the simmering uncertainty of the crowd spills over, like water bubbling on to a hotplate, creating a palpable fizz of panic.

The Reverend Silas Tate swallows and addresses my mother. 'Take my carriage,' he says. 'It will accommodate at least seven.'

And then we run.

There is a strange sort of silence in the moments after a disaster, pierced only by the weeping of those that have lost the ones they love.

It was Henry Fisher, Bertie's pa, who first noticed the water trickling through a rock face a few days ago, and so they'd stopped working that seam while they waited for it to dry out, like it usually did. There was no cause for alarm. They'd use the time to see to some routine maintenance of the tunnels and coal trucks.

On Sunday morning, Henry arrived very early at the mine with Bertie skipping along beside him.

The carts for repair were bunched together at the bottom of the shaft, so Henry winched two men, Arthur Davis and Gerald Puddy, down in the cage, leaving Bertie up top. Bertie was too young to be allowed down too, which annoyed him greatly. He loved the bawdy chatter of the miners and hated to miss out, and so occasionally his father would give in and let him ride up and down with the men in the cage, in the misplaced hope that it would somehow put Bertie off the idea of being a miner. Today, though, Henry sent Bertie home; the men needed to get on and the boy would only be in the way. Bertie complained bitterly and it had taken a sharp clip round the ear for him to leave.

Afterwards, wrapped in a blanket and shivering with more than cold, Henry couldn't say what had made him recheck that seam. The two men had been down the pit working on the trucks for an hour or more when he went down to look. When Henry saw that the trickle had become a surge, pumping out water with the flow of a fist-width pipe, he shouted down the shaft to the others, warning them to get to the cage and come up. His shouts were swallowed up in the sudden thunder-crack of splitting rock.

Henry ran, leaping into the dark, a sharp pain in his wrist as he grabbed the chain of the cage just as the vein exploded behind him and water spewed through the tunnel. It roared down into the shaft, angry and black and thick with coal dust, like the monstrous inky spurt of the kraken. Arthur Davis, caught in the shaft with Gerald, said they'd thought the whole mine was falling in, such was the noise, and the two of them had ducked and covered their heads with their arms, an instinctive but futile action.

Water plummeted into the pit, dousing and smashing every lamp in petty fury, throwing endless darkness into its depths, hitting the men as a solid mass, slamming them off their feet. Immediately it was up to their waists, churning and spewing, dragging them away from the sides of the pit as they grappled and clawed for something to hold on to. Arthur grabbed a handrail and Gerald grasped desperately at Arthur's waist-jacket but could gain no purchase on it, the leather slick and oily.

Gerald went under, screaming for his mother.

Arthur, inch by painstaking inch, made his way alone to the cage, guided by a steady, deliberate *clang, clang* – later discovered to be Henry, still clinging to the cage chain, rhythmically kicking out his steel-capped boot – and, when Arthur got there, he hauled himself up on to it. There they sat,

Arthur and Henry, out of the water, shivering and coughing on the top of the cage.

They clung to each other for warmth and comfort, as slowly, slowly the roar of the water subsided as the pressure on the perished seam relaxed with the turn of the tide in the Severn Estuary. They would have to wait until someone missed them and raised the alarm. They both knew that would not be until nightfall, some hours away, and, heaven alone knows, could they last until then? Could Henry climb up the chain . . .? But, no, he could not, his wrist quite ruined. He cursed himself for sending Bertie home.

Bertie. Henry didn't know then that his son hadn't gone home when he'd been told to, that instead he'd waited until his father's back was turned and climbed down into the cage. How he *hated* to miss out!

It would be some hours before they found him, small and broken, curled like a sycamore leaf under the water at the bottom of the cage. Pa went to him, held him as best he could, his head against his shoulder as if asleep. And then, as three men wept, the siren wailed, although not one of those men sounded it.

*

We lay out the bodies.

One man, one boy.

It is no longer safe for me here in the village. Graffiti has appeared, seemingly overnight: every poster defaced with *Peggy Devona must burn! Kill all creepers!*

So after the funerals I am to leave, with the shrieks and cries of 'Creeper! Creeper!' from our neighbours, our friends, ringing in my ears.

Mr Bletchley has offered me a refuge – the Psychic Emporium will be my new home. Pa tells me that it won't be for long, and he will be waiting for me when I return to the village. Mama is broken – the fact she has agreed to this plan shows she must be scared, but she's trying to show so much courage. And so must I, for although my life is now under threat, there is someone else I must save. I have to. I can't lose anyone else.

I'm coming for you, Sally.

BRISTOL

We arrive in Bristol after dusk, just as the sky is dipping its fingers in coal dust to slowly smudge away the light of the day. The journey from home has seemed endless, tracing the dark twist of the River Avon for hours until the Clifton Suspension Bridge rears into view. I'm further away from home than I've ever been before.

'Not bad, eh?' Mr Bletchley bangs on the roof of the carriage with a silver-tipped cane. 'Pull over, Jeffries – let's show her off!'

My heart sinks. I'm in no mood for admiring this feat of engineering, although it's a relief to finally stop; for all its button-backed upholstery, the carriage is no smoother to ride in than a hay wagon and the motion has stirred up my innards like curds in a butter churner.

The bridge is like a harp, sliced and thrown from one side of the Avon Gorge to the other. Ignoring Mr Bletchley's boasting – you would think he had built the thing himself – I get out of the carriage to stretch my legs and have a closer look. And then I feel the familiar tingle on my scalp, the thud in my temples. Someone is calling me.

'I've been waiting,' says a voice when I reach the water's edge. 'We all have.'

All?

I pull back my gaze. They are everywhere, or at least, in that moment, that's how it seems: spirits tumbling in the brown, foaming water, arms reaching as if to grab me. I skitter backwards on the gravel, terrified in case *something* lunges at me, then I run full pelt back to the carriage, into which I stumble.

Mr Bletchley's face shifts from confused to concerned. 'Go, go, GO!' he shouts, thwacking the carriage roof with his cane. The horses whinny and rear and we're off, shaking around like two dice in a cup.

He asks me, some moments later when my breath has returned, what it was that happened – what did

I see? But I can't answer him, for how could I even begin to explain that in the water I saw scores of people? Dead ones. Good and bad. *Waiting.*

It makes sense, I suppose. There are a thousand times more people here in the city than in our tiny village. Which means a thousand times more deaths, and a thousand times more spirits. Were all those spirits I saw on their burn? Do *that* many people die here, every day?

Thinking logically doesn't stop my hands from shaking, however, and we finish the last part of the journey in silence, until Mr Bletchley informs me that we are minutes away from our destination. We are close to fashionable Park Street, about half a mile from the cathedral, and twice that distance from the zoo, where an elephant called Zebi has a reputation for eating straw hats. Beckford Square looms proudly over the muddle of the city below.

My bedroom, on the very top floor of number seven, is the smallest in the house. It has pointed eaves, and a neat window set into the slope of the ceiling that I have to stand on tiptoe to see out of.

It will soon be as dark as pitch outside but Mr Bletchley assures me I have the very best view, so

I take a look. I can see the houses opposite – terraced and honey-coloured, each with eight leaded sash windows and a glossy double front door fitted with a shiny brass knocker. In the middle of the square there's a well-tended, fence-edged green space, and if I press my nose to the glass there is Brandon Hill, from the top of which, according to Mr Bletchley, you can see the whole of Bristol. If I could get up there, I could work out where the gaol is, where Sally is. *Oh, Sally!* My heart lurches. To think of her in a cold, gloomy cell . . . I can't bear it. I simply can't. I *must* see her! I must help her!

I also need to get to Clifton Lodge. If I could speak to Lady Stanton's spirit and find out what really happened to her . . . But what then? I really don't know. So far, though, it's all the plan I have.

I make a note in my little journal, which Mama covered for me in strong blue cotton ticking, stitching the material into a neatly fitting dust jacket. '"Knowledge is power", Mama,' I'd parroted back at her when she saw what I was up to. 'Quite right,' she replied, a smile twitching her lips, 'but best we keep this between us, as I'm not sure it applies to your father, in this instance.'

I press the diary to my nose and breathe in, the faint scent of home making me sad, but giving me strength too. I tuck it back under the rest of my things, burying it out of sight. You can't be too careful, especially in the big city.

Looking around me I see it's a pretty room, recently decorated. The putty-coloured walls are clean and bright, and I have a washbasin and fireplace, a small desk and chair, and a brass-framed bed with a white coverlet embroidered with tiny sprigs of blue flowers. It's a relief to find myself in such cheerful surroundings, for my troubled state after the incident at the bridge had been further rattled by what greeted me as we arrived at my new home.

On the outside, number seven looks the same as the other houses on the square, handsome and neat and respectable. But inside it's . . . unusual.

I didn't notice *how* unusual at first, my head turned as it was by the grand staircases and wood-panelled walls, the table-sized chandeliers dripping in glass and crystal. It really is the grandest house I have ever seen. The ceiling cornices are decorated with plaster ribbons and swags, and the floors covered in oriental rugs. The walls are painted in burgundy, sky blue and mint green; there is colour everywhere.

Mr Bletchley offered details – here were the main reception rooms, the formal dining room; there was the door to his private quarters, over here the door to the kitchens. He pointed out the indoor privy and proudly described the new sewerage system in alarming detail. 'This house – the whole square, in fact – is built on the site of an old workhouse,' he informed me. 'I suspect our facilities are a trifle more luxurious than theirs would have been, wouldn't you think?'

We made our way up the stairs to the first floor, the soft light from the gas lamps set in gleaming brass sconces illuminating the walls. With my foot on the last step I had the sensation of walking from day to night and rubbed at my sleep-filled eyes, thinking at first that the lamps had suddenly dimmed. I glanced behind me; the hallway below was still bright and inviting, but ahead the walls were painted in moody, chalky-textured shades the colours of stormy nights, angry seas and deep, ancient forests. For a moment my legs hesitated, reluctant to continue. As Mr Bletchley and I stepped on to the landing, what seemed like a thousand faces stared back at me, their twisted features screaming silently from the walls. I realized they were strange masks, elaborately decorated and terrifying, some beaded and jewelled, some with sharp, hooked beaks ready to peck at you should you turn your back.

'Antiques, the masks,' commented Mr Bletchley. 'Aren't they marvellous?'

I nodded as his voice brought me back to myself.

'This is where the clients of the emporium wait.' Mr Bletchley waved towards a neat semicircle of plush velvet sofas and chairs in the open area to our right. 'The spinning wheel was salvaged from the workhouse before it was torn down,' he said.

The item was almost lost in the dark but I could just make it out: a simple wooden wheel and treadle used by countless women and children in the past, carrying out relentless hours of finger-pinching work in return for bed and board. An innocuous-looking piece of wood, and yet it gave me chills, like everything here. And something was next to it. A dark shape. I blinked, hard. What was it? A shadow? A person? A . . . child? I blinked again. Nothing, it was nothing. I scolded myself for letting my imagination run away with me, as if any imagination were needed to supplement the strangeness of this place.

Next to the spinning wheel was a large ebony cabinet. It was lit only by the light from a smoked-glass lamp set on a small, round table with legs shaped like serpents. It was little wonder that I thought my eyes were playing tricks on me. When they finally became accustomed to the half-light I saw the cabinet was full of glass bell jars teeming with disturbing objects, curiosities suspended in formaldehyde no doubt designed to horrify: a piglet with two heads, a tiny hairless rat, and various other malformed, unrecognizable monstrosities.

'Why?' I asked, unable to tear my eyes away. It wasn't just the jars; the shelves groaned with lifeless creatures that once crawled, slunk, flew, scuttled and hopped, now forever immobile. Creatures were pinned and glued and stuffed and trussed, some as in life, but others facing eternity in an unnatural pose, such as the kitten standing upright playing cricket, a tiny cricket bat stapled to its paw.

The right to dignity in death is not for every creature, it seems.

We continued walking, passing two sets of double doors, for which, in spite of all his previous commentary, Mr Bletchley offered no mention.

'Here we are,' he said, coming to a stop at the end of the hallway. I couldn't see what 'here' was at first, but when I looked more closely at where he was gesturing, I saw that we'd come to a door that you'd barely notice unless you knew it was there.

'This goes up to your room.'

Photographs surrounded the door, and some were on the door itself. Light spots danced in my eyes when I glanced at them. *Was it the reflection of candles? No.* I looked, properly looked, at them. A sea of faces stared back at me; there were family groups, individual portraits, some formal, some more casual, and on most a smudge of light, no bigger than a child's thumbprint, shining down from the photographs like a thousand softly twinkling stars.

What is this place?

Later that night I drift in and out of sleep. I'd stayed in my room after Mr Bletchley had shown me the stairs to it; I'd been too exhausted for supper. Now, dreams and wakefulness twisted and tangled, melding until I don't know what's real and what's imagined. We were numb, after the accident, and me leaving the village was the result of an understanding between myself, Mama and Pa. It was *mostly* an unspoken agreement, except Mama had plenty to say about Mr Bletchley in the short time we all had together before I left.

'We have no choice now; the village is no longer safe for you, Peggy, and you must get away from here, and quickly. But, heavens to Betsy, I wish it could be anywhere but *there*,' she'd said.

'Yes, Mama.'

'They're a funny lot, city folk – keep your wits about you, my girl.'

'Yes, Ma.'

'They're charlatans, that lot at the emporium. Not a whiff of the whisperling skill between them, not like you, Pegs. To think that Bletchley's badgered us for years to get you to work for him, and now he's got his way! Just don't get yourself dragged into their games!'

'I won't, Ma! You don't have to say it ten thousand times!'

I am the last person to defend Mr Bletchley, but in this instance I wonder if Ma – and Pa, for that matter, who hung back, nodding along – will be wrong. No matter how many times I insisted that I would definitely not work for Bletchley and would only accept his offer of refuge, nothing more, Mama's thin-lipped expression suggested that she thought me quite deluded. I'm fairly sure that the crackle of her irritation was really to mask her upset, for the strength of our last hug was such that as I stir and turn over in my strange new bed I can smell the trace of her perfume upon my scarf as I cuddle it for comfort.

In my dreams I'm in the parlour back home, cross-legged on the rug in front of the unlit fire, Wolf as ever at my side. I'm younger, nine or ten, and I'm reading the Book of Devona and I am full of fear.

'What are you doing?' Pa asks, jolting me from my study.

'It says horrible things, Pa! Terrible things! I don't want to be like this any more!' I tap at the open page, running my fingers over the damp-swollen paper. I read aloud, fearfully: '"Whirling phantoms accompany me always, not a hair's breadth from mine eyes, eternally waiting for a conduit to slip through." Is that right, that they're always here? What is a conduit? Am *I* a conduit? Are they slipping through me right now, Pa?'

Pa's face is rigid with fury. 'For pity's sake, Peggy, leave the book alone! I told you, you weren't ready to read it!'

'I'm sorry, Pa, but I want to know!' I sob into my hands and kick at the book, sending it skidding across the parlour floor.

'Peggy!' Pa strides over and tenderly picks it up as if it were a newborn. 'You know how precious this book is, not only to us, but to every future Devona woman and her protectors. It's our bible, Peg. You must respect it!'

'I *do* respect it, Pa! But it's about me and I wanted to know!' I take a breath. 'It shouldn't be the menfolk that do all the learning.'

He narrows his eyes. 'Have you been speaking to your mother?'

'No,' I lie.

Now in my dreams Pa sits next to me, cross-legged on the parlour floor, cradling the book on his lap. 'Of course you should read it for yourself, Peg, but the time must be right. You're still coming to terms with your skills and it would be too much to take on, at your age. This proves my point. I told you not to open it but you went ahead, and now you're upset. I bet you wish you hadn't read it now, don't you?'

I consider this. At first glance the book did terrify me. But now . . . I stubbornly jut out my chin. 'I want to know. Even the bad stuff. I have to learn.'

Pa covers his mouth with his hand, but it's too late – I notice the dimpling of his cheek. 'Pa! Don't laugh at me!'

'I'm sorry, Peg, I'm not laughing, not really. I'm . . . proud. Very proud.' He pushes the book from his lap, reaches over and pulls me next to him, folding me into a hug. 'Ask me anything. What do you want to know?'

'Are there really spirits around me all the time?'

'I don't know, Peg, and that's the truth. We don't know if everything in the book is entirely fact. It would be different if there were a living Devona we could ask, one who has the gift, but in this generation it's only you.'

'That isn't helpful, Pa.'

'Well, how about this, then?' He slides the book carefully in front of his crossed legs and scans the passage. 'It's a highly unlikely set of circumstances that will actually allow you to enter the realm of — what was it?'

'Whirling phantoms.'

'Yes, that. So, even if it were true, it just can't happen.'

'It said something about holding hands?'

'That's only part of it.'

'But —'

'Trust me, Peg. If you ever encounter anything that makes you fearful, fill your head with other thoughts so there isn't room for anything unwelcome. Push it away! There are other ways too, but we'll come to that when –'

'*When I'm ready,*' I mimic, allowing myself a smile.

Pa grins at me. 'Very good, you're learning. Here, let's practise.' He sticks his fingers in his ears and sings, 'La-la-la-la-*laah*! We can't hear you, terrible whirling things!'

I giggle in my dream and I'm still smiling when I wake. 'Pa?' But he isn't here, of course, and a now familiar weight returns to my chest as I remember where I am and why.

I hear a commotion – voices float up the stairs: women's voices, eager and excited. I shake myself fully awake and creep to the door.

'I don't understand – how did it happen?'

'Did you see it, Mary? Did you?'

'She *became* him; I'm sure of it.'

'But did it feel . . . Was it as if . . .?'

'Oh, Lillian, it did! It really did!'

'Miss Richmond, we can't thank you enough!'

A third voice, cool and gentle, balm-like over the other two: 'Why, Mrs Proctor, you have no need to thank me. It was an honour to be part of your reconnection with your loved one. Truly, I don't think I've ever experienced such a pure, almost *sacred* moment of love such as that. I feel –' her voice cracks – 'blessed to have been part of it.'

'And you're certain you won't take any more money?' says one of the other women, Mrs Proctor, presumably. 'A guinea seems too little for what you've done for me.'

'No, absolutely not. I won't hear of it.'

'You're an angel, Miss Richmond, a real angel. We can't tell you what it means to have found you. We are forever in your debt.'

A quiet sigh. 'No, dear ladies, it's I who am in yours. I once thought my gift was a burden, but you have given me fresh purpose. I am humbled to have been in the presence of such enduring love. Now, please excuse me, ladies, for I am quite wearied and need to rest awhile.'

I swallow a scoff. I'll bet ten a'penny Miss Richmond is even holding the back of her hand against her forehead by now. *What a ridiculous performance!*

'Of course, of course,' urge Lillian Proctor and her companion. 'Please forgive us, Miss Richmond! Until next week?'

'Yes. Until next week. I'll have your photograph delivered when it's ready.'

'Oh! How wonderful! I'm already counting the moments until we meet again!'

It's clear Mary and Lillian are giddy with excitement, but Miss Richmond is an out-and-out charlatan, of that I'm certain. I wait until the swish of skirts and bubbles of chatter disperse before I sneak down the stairs and peek through the door at the bottom, leaning heavily into the wall in an attempt to be as invisible as possible.

'There you are, little mouse. I wondered when you would come out of your hole.'

The door is flung open before I can run back up the stairs. The lady before me is luminous; her blonde hair is curled and pinned at the nape of her neck, less fussy than is fashionable and all the more striking for it. Her dress – the colour of the deepest ocean, gleaming blue-black with a sheen that I swear I can see my face in – is fitted on the bodice and pulled in tight at the waist, giving her the figure of a dress-maker's mannequin. I tug self-consciously at my nightdress. I've never felt more like a child.

'Come, let me look at you. Margaret, isn't it?' Miss Richmond – for that is whom I presume she is – opens her arms to encourage me towards her and I step closer as if drawn by a magnet. Her accent is clipped and upper class and I see she is far younger than I pictured her, no more than eighteen or nineteen. This only makes me feel even dowdier. I doubt I'll reach such sophistication in less than half a dozen years' time!

'It's Peggy,' I say. 'People call me Peggy.'

She leans in and tucks a strand of hair behind my ear. 'Well, I shall call you Margaret, as befits such a pretty young lady.' Her hand is cool against my cheek and she slides it down, under my chin, tipping my face up so she can examine me further. 'Yes, perfect,' she says, almost to herself. 'Attractive, but innocent. Do you ever roll your hair?'

'Um, no, not really . . . I mean, my mother has done it for me sometimes, for fun, but . . .'

'Don't,' she says sharply. 'Best you look your age. We'll do something to it, of course, but it's good. Long and wavy and –' she lifts a lock of my hair and holds it close to her eye – 'black. It's actually *black*. Like a raven's wing. Quite remarkable. Now, those eyes, let me . . . Oh!' She pouts theatrically. 'Well, that's a little disappointing. I was hoping for something dramatic, like azure or emerald – or violet! But yours are –' she tips my head up to the lamplight – 'disappointingly normal.'

'My pa says they are the colour of nature, blue and green and grey –'

'And your pa is right, of course! But that isn't really enticing enough for the advertisement boards.'

Advertisement boards?

'Well, never mind!' she trills. 'We can't have everything! Very good, all things considered, although you could do with wearing something a little less . . . rural. Have you brought any other clothes with you?'

'Well, this *is* my nightgown,' I say, before considering her question. I have one piece of luggage with me: a carpet bag filled with underclothes and two pinafores, my precious journal and a pencil, and my Sunday-best dress. This last item is a cut-down frock of my mother's in the deepest sapphire-blue, full skirted, with a fitted waist and high, lace-ruffled neck, and tiny mother-of-pearl buttons at the back. *What a waste of good packing space*, I thought. I could have brought at least two books with me if I'd left it at home, but Mama insisted I have something for 'best'.

A copy of *The Englishwoman's Domestic Magazine* was left in my room and I now regret looking through it. I am a village mouse with village clothes and hair.

My pinafores are plain and old and out of fashion; even my best Sunday dress is the wrong shape.

Too bad. 'I have a very nice dark-blue dress,' I say, defensive of Mama and her outmoded hand-me-down. I swallow the threat of tears. Who cares what some silly woman in London with nothing better to do says about the 'appropriate size of bustles'.

Miss Richmond claps her hands in delight. 'Well, that sounds perfect. We can try it later.'

'Um, Miss . . . Richmond? What's all this about?'

'Please, call me Cecily. Did Mr Bletchley not explain?'

I shake my head and Cecily laughs, showing a row of small, perfect white teeth.

'Oh, Margaret, I'm so sorry – you must think me quite dreadful!'

'No, of course not, I'm just a bit . . .'

'Confused? I'm not surprised in the slightest. Let me explain. You're to be my new assistant and we shall start work post-haste.'

'We shall?'

Cecily snakes an arm round my shoulders. 'We most certainly shall, my dear. And from what I hear, with my skills and your particular talents, you and I are about to make an absolute killing.'

By the time I'm back in my room, a cold lump has settled in the pit of my stomach. *So, Mama was right!* Traitor Bletchley has lured me here under false pretences, not out of a sense of duty to our family or concern for me, but to exploit my skill for his own ends! How *dare* he! How will I *bear* it?

I fall asleep eventually, overcome by a deep exhaustion. As soon as I wake, late in the morning, that sense of betrayal is with me again. While I sulk, Mrs Morris, the housekeeper – a squat woman, solid as a sideboard and about as personable – invites me to breakfast in the kitchen as I missed the formal sitting.

'Help yourself to more tea if you want,' she says. 'Don't be standing on ceremony waiting for me to pour it or you'll be as dry as a camel's hump come Christmas.'

This is about as friendly as she gets, but I don't mind. I like it here. It's a comfier space than the rest of the house above with its strange mixture of elegance and carefully curated terror. On my way downstairs I paused to look at the photographs again. Today they look perfectly normal; I must have imagined the lights. They were probably a reflection from the lamps on the landing.

Here in the kitchen, copper pots hang on hooks over a huge ebony-black cast-iron range. According to Mrs Morris, there's always something bubbling away: at the very least a pot of porridge in the morning, from which I'm instructed to ladle myself a bowl, and a stockpot in the afternoon, usually next to a kettle boiling, or an iron heating, ready to fill the air with puffs of starchy clouds as it presses the laundry cranked down from the airer.

I run a finger over the kitchen table, which is large, solid and gnarly, a giant version of the one at home in our cottage. Homesickness kicks me in the guts, even though I've been gone less than a day. I'd like to stay down here until I can leave, whenever that may be.

Mrs Morris is helped by Dotty, the maid; it's little wonder she's whip thin and shorter than me because she's worked into the ground! Dotty seems to do everything, including the cooking, and all under Mrs Morris's watchful eye. I'm pleased to see someone more my own age, but she looks at me as if I have two heads. I don't think she likes me.

The housekeeper's bell rings, causing Dotty to jump. Mrs Morris tuts. 'One of these days, people'll learn how to get their own drinks and I can sit down for five minutes,' she mutters, creaking to her feet and dragging off her mob cap. 'You make sure you get all them potatoes peeled for dinner, Dotty. And no filling her head –' nodding towards me – 'with any of your tall tales,' she warns. 'She's a guest, and a child at that. When you've finished the spuds, make a start on them,' she says, indicating a brace of pheasant, and she shuffles out.

The room falls into awkward silence.

'Here, let me help,' I say, taking one of the birds.

'You know what ye're doin'?' Dotty sounds suspicious. 'There's a knack to it, you know.' She pushes the pan of potatoes to one side, wipes her hands on her apron and picks up the other bird, eyeing me levelly. 'You ain't one of *them*, are ya?'

'One of what?'

'A creeper – whisperling – medium . . . whatever they calls themselves, makes no odds to me.'

'Why would you think that?'

'Why else would the master have brought you here?'

'He didn't *bring* me – I'm not livestock,' I retort. 'I'm . . . a relation. I came of my own accord. I have business in Bristol; that's why I'm here.'

'Oh, *business*, is it? I heard you had to get out of your village before they strung you up and burned you at the stake.' She smiles, mocking me, bending one of the lower legs of the pheasant at the joint, her face reddening with the effort. The leg gives with a dull *snap*.

'How do you know . . .? Anyway, it wasn't like that.' Except it very nearly was. I push away the memories of the villagers, our friends and neighbours, stepping away from me, whispering and fearful in the days before I left. Tears spring up and I wipe my eyes on my sleeve.

'Don't get upset on account of me,' says Dotty. 'I don't mean nothin' by it. We're a bit cannier here in the city –' she taps her nose – 'not like those bumpkins who believe all sorts of guff. The number of people Mr Bletchley's had workin' here with their seances and spells, thinkin' they're gifted!' She rolls her eyes. 'Don't worry – once he realizes you're no more a creeper than I am, you'll be back in your own bed before you know it ... after you've attended to your *business*, of course.' She looks me square in the eye as she tugs stringy tendons from the leg of the bird.

I glare at Dotty. 'Plucked or skinned?' I say, snipping the head off my pheasant at the base of its neck.

Dotty raises an eyebrow and gives a slow smile. 'Well, well, well. If you're going to make yourself useful, then I think it's time for a brew. You can tell me all about this business of yours and I'll tell you about those two little madams upstairs.'

Wait – there are *two* of them?

Dotty describes the parlour where the 'little madams' work as groaning with strange artefacts – shrunken heads and foul-smelling potions, little dolls stuck with pins that there's 'no way in a month of Sundays' she'll ever be dusting. I wonder why she is scared of something she's so certain is bobbins, but know better than to ask.

She is getting into her stride when a wallop from Mrs Morris with a half-plucked pheasant silences her. Scares Dotty half to death, by the look on her face, but, still, I am cheered. Dotty has told me lots about the local area. She's given me some gruesome bits of information: where Amelia Dyer, the baby strangler, lived; where so-and-so was squished by a horse and cart and how their head 'popped like an over-ripe marrow'; how many people jump from the bridge each year (this cheerful nugget chilled me the most, after seeing all those desperate souls in the water). She's also suggested a charming walk from here to Leigh Woods, where there is an Iron Age fort, lovely views over the Avon Gorge, and a jolly little tea shop that serves delicious drop scones. And she's given me one *very* useful piece of information too: in mentioning a few landmarks to look out for on the way to the tea shop, she included Clifton Lodge, which means I can put at least part of my plan into action now that I know Lady Stanton's spirit is within walking distance. I just have to get away from Mr Bletchley (Whisperling Traitor of the Highest Order!), who has insisted I take lunch with him.

I glare at him from across a table that is as long as our cottage is wide and as glossy as golden syrup. He is reading a newspaper, harrumphing occasionally in either disgust or amusement, I can't tell which. Eventually he folds the paper into quarters and places it on the table with a sigh. 'I know you're cross with me, Peggy, but I had to tell my staff something. They didn't know I had any remaining family, let alone a niece who is a whisperling. This way you're just one of my potential clairvoyants. I made no mention of your genuine gifts, I assure you. The fewer people who know the truth about the Devonas, the better.'

My jaw tightens. 'You are ashamed of us – me, Mama and Pa.'

'That could not be further from the truth,' he says, but I must have hit a nerve for his face flushes as if he has stubbed his toe. 'You have the same expression of righteous indignation as your father, you know.'

'Do not speak of my father. He is an honourable man and you are not. You have lured me here under false pretences.'

'Not everything is black or white, Peggy. Not everything is right or wrong.'

I clench my hands into fists and squeeze my eyes tight, fighting back tears of anger and sorrow. At the mention of Pa, homesickness barrels in again, for, like it or not, Mr Bletchley is the connection between Bristol and the village, and when I see him, I think of Mama and Pa. And when I think of them, I want to leave this house and run all the way back home. 'Why did you tell Dotty what happened in Alderley, about the villagers running me out?' I ask angrily. 'She suspects me to be . . . what I am.'

'I told her no such thing!' he snaps. 'As if it would be right for me to tell that slip of a girl anything at all – she is one of the domestic staff, and a junior one at that. I've told no one. You must be mistaken, Peggy.'

I'm not mistaken, but there's little point in arguing. 'You speak of right and wrong, Mr Bletchley, but what could possibly be right about what's happened to Sally?' I nod to his newspaper, with its headline about Bristol Gaol being full to bursting. 'Sally is in there, and she hasn't done anything wrong.' It kills me to think of her in there with the rats, the cold, and the terrible fear of what is to come. 'We *must* seek her release. It's why I agreed to stay here,' I croak, swallowing down a tangy mixture of tears and bile. 'To save Sally. Please, Mr Bletchley, you have contacts . . . Will you help me?'

'Agreed? As memory serves, you came here because your neighbours were sharpening their pitchforks and coming after you. Besides, it's not that straightforward. I can't simply get her out, just like that.'

'Can I at least visit her? Make sure she's all right and ask her what happened?'

'I . . . I'm not sure that's such a good idea,' he replies. 'You would need a visitor's order and you're too young for one of those – and just as well, in my opinion. Prison is no place for a chi–'.

He stops himself, but the truth hangs between us. He's right – prison is *no* place for a child, and yet Sally is there, and she's not the only one either.

'Very well,' I say. 'I was also thinking of going to Clifton Lodge in the hope I could – oh, I don't know – perhaps make contact with Lady Stanton. There'd be no harm in that, surely? You can't expect me to do nothing.'

He raises a grey, woolly eyebrow. 'So I'm beginning to learn, my dear. I understand your keenness, but I must implore you not to get involved. Leave it to the authorities. Your meddling won't help anything at all.'

Meddling? 'I want to help my best friend!' I reply angrily. 'They're going to hang her and she didn't do anything. She's fourteen and she's innocent and they're going to kill her! I have to do *something*.'

He swallows and fiddles with his collar. 'Well, yes, fourteen *is* terribly young. If she didn't do it, the truth will come out in the trial. There's no need for you to draw attention to yourself. Please, Peggy – promise me you won't.'

'Stuff drawing attention to myself! This isn't about me. We have to *do something* for Sally! The judge will see some poor servant girl whose family haven't got two ha'pennies to rub together. They'll say she's guilty and that'll be the end of her.' A sob spools up from my chest and I swallow it down, hard. 'How about you lend me some money? Please? I could pay for a lawyer for Sally! Miss Richmond – Cecily . . . I met her last night. She seems very nice really and I promise to do lots of good . . . "seancing".'

Mr Bletchley smiles tightly. 'Leave it to the grown-ups, there's a good girl. I didn't bring you here for you to get yourself into more trouble.'

A rush of fury burns in my chest and my choked tears burst through the dam. 'Grown-ups are *idiots*!' I scream, sobbing angrily, scraping back my chair and running from the dining room.

I slam my bedroom door shut and throw myself on the bed, punching and kicking the mattress and pillows until, leaden-limbed, I sit up and hold my pounding head in my hands. My carpet bag peeks out from under the bed. My heart thuds. *I pushed that further under*, I think. I *know* I pushed it out of sight, away from prying eyes. I pull it right out, into the middle of the floor, turn it upside down and shake it empty. Nothing is missing, but I'm unsettled. Unsettled but determined. I wipe my eyes with the back of my hand.

So what if the grown-ups won't help? So what if the authorities won't listen?

I'll just have to do it my way, won't I?

Thud thud thud.

I'm knocking at the gnarled, church-like door of Clifton Lodge.

Thud thud thud.

No answer. I knock harder, knuckles bruising on the knotted wood.

Thud thud thud.

I'm coming for you, Sally, let me in!

Thud thud thud.

But Sally isn't here, is she? She's in gaol.

Thud thud thud.

You couldn't get to Lady Stanton's today, remember? You have to go tomorrow.

Thud thud thud.

You're asleep! Wake up, wake up!

Thud thud thud.

I'm half awake now, but the knocking still slips into my woolly head. I check the small brass carriage clock on the bedside table; it's just after eleven at night.

Thud thud thud.

Is it someone at my door? I haven't left my room since the scene at lunchtime. Perhaps someone is checking on me.

Thud thud thud.

No, it's too muffled to be someone outside my room. It sounds more like . . . a cane knocking against the floor in a room below.

And then: *Aaaaagh!*

I sit up, fully awake now, trying to still the nervous fluttering in my tummy, straining to hear over the roaring throb of blood in my ears. That was definitely a scream, no doubt about it, and now there's a groaning noise and the faintest *ting* of a bell. Chanting. Someone is chanting. A low, steady incantation that pounds in my chest, like the thrum of a steam train pulling into a station.

Yes, it's definitely coming from below. Mr Bletchley has his quarters on the ground floor, close to the indoor bathroom, and I'm yet to hear so much as a peep from him, in spite of him being the most extraordinarily loud man, so it can't be him.

I have to take a look. I slide out of bed, cursing as my foot narrowly misses my chamber pot. Opening the bedroom door as noiselessly as I can, I creep down the steep, uncarpeted stairs and gently unlatch the door to the landing, keen not to draw the attention of Cecily again. The longer I can avoid her, the longer I can side-step becoming her assistant.

The chanting noise is louder from my spot here on the attic stairs; it's definitely coming from the room next to Cecily's and for a moment I hesitate, remembering what Dotty said about shrunken heads and pickled innards. Could it be witchcraft? *Real* magic? It seems unlikely, even in this supposedly liberal city. Surely any actual witches would be too wary to put on a public show? Wouldn't they?

I pad along the landing, creep past Cecily's rooms, and tiptoe up to the second door, inching forward until my left hand rests on its frame. From here, the waiting area is visible, tonight lit only by candlelight. The spinning wheel casts strange dancing shadows on the black-flocked wallpaper, the strange, unsettling bell-jar creatures reanimated by the flicker and flit of flames. How sad to be more vibrant in death than in life!

Slowly, slowly I lean in to the door, turning my head until my ear is but a hair's breadth away from the narrow gap around the frame. The glossed-white door is cool against my cheek. I inch my way down towards the handle. If there's no key in the lock on the other side, I may be able to peek in. There's a smell – incense of some sort – misting under the door and pooling into a haze on the landing. I swallow a cough, and freeze. Did they hear me? No, it doesn't seem they did ... The chanting is so constant that I have to concentrate to unravel it from silence; it has become background noise, the heartbeat of whatever is going on in there.

Thud thud thud.

The thrum pulsating from inside the room mixes with the warm, spicy tang of the incense ... and why am I so *sleepy*? My eyelids feel as if I've had lead sewn into my lashes and I stretch my eyes open in an effort to stay awake. I'm almost there, moving slowly so as not to knock my knees against the door or rattle the bone-white handle with my elb–

Clunk ... The doorknob judders and I fall

backwards, slippers catching on my babyish nightgown as I scrabble to stay on my feet. But already chairs are scraping and footsteps approaching and then a bag is thrown over my head and something is pressing against my face and it smells of sweet, rotten leaves and I can't breathe, I can't breathe . . .

I was drugged, I think, by some weird-smelling liquid on a cloth held over my mouth and nose. I catch scattered, meaningless snatches of conversation, words being written down, pages ripped apart and thrown into the air, strewn out of order.

'*Miraculous! . . . Can I touch her? . . . Astonishing! . . . She's among us . . . astounding . . . the evidence of my own eyes . . . truly phenomenal . . . Will she speak? . . . Will you put the lights up?*'

There's a drumbeat, loud and insistent, flashes of light, screams, shouts and confusion, then pitch-black as I'm dragged roughly and pushed into a small space. (*A box? Cupboard? Oh goodness . . . a coffin?*) A finger presses to my lips and a harsh '*Shhhh!*' is hissed into my ear. And then I hear a click as a door is closed and it is silent. I am alone and I don't move, daren't speak and wonder if I shall die here.

But then . . .

'Gi'ssa glass a water, quick!'

'Was that really necessary, Ceci?'

'Don't 'ave a benny on me, Oti! What would you 'ave done? 'Ave her ruin everything? Better she appears as a ghost-babber with a veil chucked on 'er 'ead than 'ave her blunder in and mess it all up.'

'I know, but really she's just a child and goodness knows what that stuff'll do to her insides!'

'Oh bobbins, Oti – she'll be fine. They use it all the time these days.'

'*Doctors*, Ceci. Doctors use it.'

'Oh, shut yer larrup an' give us a hand to get 'er out! An' get that yoke off 'er noggin!'

I am released, eased from my prison by gentle hands, and am guided to sit on something solid and uncomfortable, presumably the thing in which I had been confined.

A thousand clog-wearing ants are marching through my head and my mouth is so dry my lip sticks to my top teeth. I am uncovered and a glass is pressed into my hands.

Cecily cups the back of my head. ''Ere, drink this.'

I gulp it down, gratefully, and the army in my head retreats. 'What happened?' I ask. 'And why do you sound so different?'

Cecily shrugs. 'It's my old voice,' she says, back to the more refined accent I heard her speaking in last night. 'One gets taken more seriously if one sounds ... posher.' She pouts prettily. 'I tend to drop my Hs in times of stress.'

'Oh.' My eyes are becoming accustomed to the dancing light; the room is alive with the warm glow of dozens of church candles. The other girl swims into focus. Oti is as striking as Cecily, and about the same age.

'So,' she says, 'you must be Margaret. Nice to meet you, flower.' She has a slight singsong inflection.

'You're ... Welsh?' I say stupidly.

'I am that. All the time too,' she says, throwing a pointed look at Cecily, who pokes her tongue out in return.

Oti's black skin glows in the candlelight, flames catching and dancing like fireflies on the countless golden chains round her neck. Her hair is wrapped in a swathe of silky blood-red material knotted high on the top of her head, and a golden spider-shaped pendant nestles at her throat. The top of her dress is off the shoulder, wrapped and crossed low at the front, with long, voluminous sleeves nipped in and buttoned at the wrist, and the skirt is full and flowing in shades of crimson, black and gold. She wears a matching shawl in the same colours, dotted with tiny glass beads, round her shoulders. My head swims.

'Oh dear, love, you feelin' a bit groggy?' she says, leaning towards me.

'I-I'm not sure,' I stammer back. I think I feel fine, apart from being a little wobbly and headachy, like I do when I've sneaked a swig or two of brandy when clearing up after a wake, but . . . these girls, this *room* . . .

Oti sees me looking and laughs. 'You likes our office then, little one?'

I nod. The walls are panelled in dark wood, some dressed with large pieces of material that match the heavy deep-green velvet curtains; there are plush wall hangings, bookshelves stuffed with fat leather-bound tomes. Richly carved screens divide the room, and there are tall-backed, almost throne-like chairs, as well as a sideboard groaning with decanters and crystal glasses, and a large display cabinet containing strange, unsettling items that echo those in the waiting area. Details reveal themselves little by little, the flickering candlelight casting menacing shadows, increasing the eeriness tenfold. I catch sight of ornate and terrifying wooden masks, some with sharpened teeth; stuffed animals under glass domes; and a bowl containing something (could it even be *hair*?) smouldering. On a round, cloth-covered table, a silver salver is laden with curious knick-knacks (a child's shoe, a bonnet, a pipe, a pillbox, a pair of wire-rimmed spectacles). This is not a normal parlour. I locate the door, should my legs ever stop wobbling enough to hasten an escape, and then I notice a wall of family photographs, much like the ones on the landing. Wait, no. The odd angle of that head, the propping-up of limbs, that woman's blank stare – *Dead folk!* They're all photos of dead folk.

Cecily taps the back of my hand. 'They're funny things, aren't they?' 'Funny' is probably not the first word I'd have said, but I nod anyway. 'I'm sure they're a comfort to some,' she goes on, 'but I can't say I'd like any photo of my dearly departed watching over me while I sleep – what do you say, old girl?' She elbows Oti in the ribs and grins as if we're three milkmaids larking about, then she looks back at me, suddenly serious. 'Are you sure you're all right? You're not very talkative. She's not very talkative, is she, Oti?'

'Not everyone jibber-jabbers like you.' Oti stands and glides around the room, snuffing candles and turning on gas lamps. She pours some water over a cloth, wrings it out and throws it over the still-smoking bowl, which she then puts on the hearth. 'Greedy fool,' she mutters, shaking her head.

'I think they're amazing,' I say.

'What are you saying, now?' asks Oti.

'The photographs,' I say. 'You can tell that most of them were taken quite soon after death. Look, that one, there.' I point to a photograph of a woman, with a young girl, around seven or eight, sitting on her lap – a mother and her daughter, presumably. 'You can see how the woman's arm is looped round the girl's waist. They wouldn't have been able to do that if they'd left it too long. On account of the rigor mortis.' Cecily and Oti are looking at me quite peculiarly. 'What?' I say. 'What's the matter?'

'It . . . it's not quite the usual reaction,' replies Cecily.

Oh.

'Perhaps you'll like these too.' Oti passes a black satin-bound book to me. It's filled with portraits of people dressed in mourning wear, with shadowy, ghostly figures lurking ominously behind them.

'What is this?' I ask.

'It's called spirit photography,' she says. 'Ever heard of it?' I shake my head and Oti smiles at my puzzled face. 'Your man Bletchley was *obsessed*. Spent a small fortune on all the latest gubbins hoping to catch a ghost with his camera. Poor beggar was devastated when it turns out it was nothing more than a cheap trick – not that he ever admitted it to us, mind. Felt bad for him, didn't we, Ceci?' Cecily pouts and nods like a sad circus clown. '*Hundreds* of photographs he's taken over the years, and he *still* insists on taking the clients' photos. For posterity, he says.' She shrugs. 'Waste of money, if you asks me, but the punters like to have a souvenir of their time here with us. I expect you've seen more of his handiwork on the way to your room?'

I nod, hoping my frown goes unnoticed. The lights in those photos looked nothing like the obviously fake shadows in these portraits. Perhaps I've misunderstood. Perhaps, along with the wrong clothes, the wrong hair and the wrong attitude, I've also got the wrong end of the stick. I glance down again at the book and its obvious trickery. *Perhaps not.*

Oti closes the book and walks over to the photograph of the woman on the wall, peering closely. 'You know, I always thought it was the child that was dead, not the mother. The woman's eyes are open. Look, see?'

'Painted on,' I reply.

Oti looks again and pulls a face. 'That's a bit grim, isn't it? The girl's eyes are shut, though.'

I shrug. 'Probably unhappy about posing for a photograph on her dead mother's lap.'

There is silence. 'You're a funny little thing, aren't you?' says Cecily finally.

'I can see why Bletchley thought you'd make a good apprentice.' Oti tips her head on one side. 'And why he thinks you're a bit of an "odd sausage".'

Is that what he said about me? A wave of nausea barrels up from my stomach. 'I don't feel so well.'

'Quick, Oti,' cries Cecily. 'The bowl, the bowl, the bowl! There you go, babber, there you go.'

Oti tuts. 'I told you that stuff was no good for her,' she mutters.

She's not wrong.

Several minutes and a thorough vomit later, my head is clearer.

Cecily hands me a cloth to wipe my mouth and kneels on the floor in front of me. 'Sorry about putting you in there, by the way.'

She nods at the thing that I'm sitting on, which now I'm less fuzzy I see is a high-sided bench, much like a narrow church pew.

'It wasn't comfortable,' I say, shifting to one side and moving my nightgown out of the way. I lean over and run my fingers over the front of the base. There's a small metal latch on the right-hand side. Curious, I flick it up and the whole front of the base pops open. I peer inside; it's very dark, and very small.

Cecily sits back on her haunches and grimaces an apology. 'What can I say? It was an emergency.'

'An emergency?'

'We had to get rid of you. It would have –'

'Broken the spiritual flow,' finishes Oti.

'Yes, quite!' says Cecily, smiling. 'It would have broken the spiritual flow.'

'When did everyone go?' I ask.

'About a half hour ago. I said they should leave quietly so as not to, you know . . .' says Oti.

'Break the spiritual flow?' I offer, and she throws her head back and laughs.

'Yes, that's it exactly,' she says, smiling, as she retrieves a huge vase of white carnations from under the round table. 'There. That's a bit more homely, don't you think?'

I nod. 'What was in the bowl?'

'Some personal effects of the deceased. One or two . . . bodily items.'

'Yuck! Why?'

Oti shrugs. 'To add to the atmosphere. Makes it all a bit more spooky and mysterious. Tonight's clients wanted to contact their dead grandfather who started the family business. Reading between the lines, the two sisters wanted to spook their younger brother into signing over his share of the company to them. They think he's more interested in wine, women and song than running the family firm.'

'Well, I suppose there's some appeal in that,' says Cecily, walking over to the sideboard and pouring out two measures of port wine. She hands a glass to Oti with a look that for some reason makes me blush and they chink glasses. 'Down the 'atch!'

'Cheers!' Oti says back.

'Did it work?' I ask. 'And how do you know that's what they were here for? Did you contact the grandfather? But you couldn't have, could you?' I go on. 'Because you're not witches, are you? Or whisperlings. Are you . . . anything?'

Cecily sits on one of the throne-like seats, shuffling round so she's sitting on it sideways, one leg flopped over the wooden arm. 'It depends what you mean by "work",' she says, taking a large gulp of port. She's choosing her words very carefully. 'The seances we hold here are very exclusive – invitation-only. It means we know exactly who'll be in attendance, and *that* means we can do a little . . . research beforehand. We're careful not to be too specific – it doesn't do to be *too* detailed with the readings. Things should be left open to interpretation. But most sitters have faith, and that's extremely powerful. The brother didn't look wholly convinced, but it may just have been bravado. His sisters, though, they were utterly enthralled, especially when you popped by, Margaret. Believing the spirits are on their side will at the very least make the sisters act more boldly, and the feckless brother will lose confidence and consequently power. Ta-dah!' Cecily kicks her leg in the air. 'Word spreads. More and more people hear about our brilliance and our ticket price goes up and up!' She grins. 'And that brother? I truly hope they do kick him out – he's an absolute ass.'

'As for your other question,' says Oti, 'no, we're not witches. Who would be so bold to say they were, after what happens to them?'

'So, what are you?' I ask.

'We're women, love. Women that people actually listen to. And in this world, that's a gift rarer than the skill of any whisperling.'

This house is smoke and mirrors from chimney pot to cellar floor. Even the door to my attic room is almost invisible, set into the wall and ingeniously painted the same colour. Fake panels have been etched with fine brushstrokes so neat that at a distance you'd never tell the door was there. Nausea tilts me sideways as I head to it and I take a moment to breathe, relaxing as the queasy wave washes away.

I try not to look at the wall of photographs, still rattled by the book Oti had shown me. We have no such images back home in the village, photography being such a new-fangled thing. We have paintings, though, colourless little portraits of various Devona women – Aunt Kitty, Granny Vada, Cousin Frances –

who Pa has reduced to dull anecdotes with the promise that I'll read their stories in the book 'one day'. *One day, indeed!* I know there is much more to these women, for when I stare at their portraits for long enough I feel an unmistakable fizz of connection.

However, one photograph catches my eye as I go to open the door. '*Happy Days*' reads the caption at the bottom in curly copperplate. I stand back for a proper view; it's an informal composition of a couple out for a bracing walk. The man wears his top hat at a slight angle; his moustache is waxed and curled. In his hand he has an umbrella, and he's raised one foot up on a low wall in front of some railings. The woman wears a dark dress and an enormous feather-plumed hat that largely conceals her face, but somehow, in spite of this, it's obvious that she radiates pure happiness. She's a woman in love.

I hesitate, a wave of uncertainty washing over me. I step closer. The man in the photograph is definitely Mr Bletchley; that much is certain. The woman? Fear needles at my neck.

It can't be . . .

I look more carefully. *How could it be?*

But there's no denying it. The woman is my mother.

I awake at first light and dress quickly, ready to demand an explanation from Mr Bletchley. I run downstairs to the landing but the photograph has gone. In its place is a lithograph of a shadowy tree, dark and threatening.

Had I dreamed it all? I lean in to examine it. The frame is edged by a faint outline a shade or two darker than the rest of the wall, where the slightly larger frame that was there before had shielded it. This square-shaped shadow on the wall both buoys and unsettles me. Someone has swapped the pictures; I'm not imagining it.

'Somethin' the matter?' says a scratchy voice.

'Dotty! You startled me! No, no, I'm fine. Listen –'

I nod at the wall – 'was there a photograph here on this wall yesterday?'

She eyes me like I'm a bird waiting to be plucked and she's deciding which of my feathers to yank out first. 'If you thinks I've gots time for standin' an' gazin' at pictures, then you've got horse dung in yer noggin where yer brains should be.' She nods at the neatly folded pile of clothes and towels in her arms. 'Would you like me to take these up, as yer ladyship is so busy appreciatin' the art?'

It sounds more like a threat than an offer. 'No,' I say, 'I'll take them. Please, give them to me.' I reach for the linens but she shifts to one side.

'T'ain't no trouble, you being a guest an' all,' she says, taking a step towards my room.

I absolutely, definitely, do not want her to go up there. I can't shake off the feeling that someone has been through my things, although there's no way of knowing who or why. I position myself between her and the door to the attic stairs and she glares at me. I put out my hands and do my best effort at a friendly smile. 'Give them to me, Dotty. Really, it's fine, thank you.'

A door along the landing opens. 'Are you ready, Margaret?' calls Cecily.

'Ready for what?' I call back.

'Mr Bletchley said you fancied looking around the area, that you have a particular interest in Clifton Lodge. He thought we could act as your guides if you'd like us to.'

He did? 'Um, yes, I'd love to. Won't be a minute – Dotty's brought me my clean laundry so I'll be with you as soon as I've taken it up.' I hold out my hands once more. 'Thank you, Dotty,' I say firmly, and Dotty has no choice but to tetchily shove the pile of linens at me.

'Enjoy your day with the coven,' she hisses under her breath. She pauses to rub at a photograph with the corner of her apron, steps back, frowns and rubs again, tutting loudly. 'Like I 'aven't got enough to do,' she grumbles, glaring at me once more as if the grubby picture is *my* fault, before turning on her heel and stomping away, mob cap bobbing irritably. I quickly put the laundry on the stairs to my room and pull the door closed with a defiant *click*.

I turn to Cecily. 'Oh, look at you!' I cry.

Cecily is wearing a brown tweed skirt, white shirt and a scarlet gentleman's waistcoat; over these there's a long tweed greatcoat nipped at the waist, a silk handkerchief tucked into the breast pocket. She also has a ribbon-trimmed top hat and –

'Are those . . . riding boots?' I ask.

'Is it too much? I don't get out into the countryside very often and one likes to be dressed in the correct attire.'

'It's not really the countryside,' I tell her. 'You can actually see it from –'

'It's green, isn't it? There's grass. *Ergo, c'est la campagne!*' Cecily giggles, hooks an arm through mine and twirls me round. 'I'm so excited about our jaunt! I've been up for hours, practically tried on everything I own.' She stops, unhooks me and looks down at herself. 'No, you're right, you're right.' She pouts. 'It's too much. I'll change. I'm sure I 'ave something more suit–'

'No!' If she changes her outfit now, we may never get out of here. I can't lose another day. 'Really, Cecily, you look lovely.'

She pauses, grabs at her skirt and swishes it from side to side, smiling coyly. 'I do, don't I?'

'Is Oti coming with us?'

'Yes, of course . . . oh, wait!' Cecily scurries to their bedroom door. 'Oti, darling!' she shouts. 'Best leave the breeches and riding crop for another time – we don't want to draw too much attention to ourselves, do we?' She looks back at me and winks, dropping her voice to a whisper. 'She's a thoroughly good egg, but between you and me she can be a little clueless, sartorially.'

'Oi! I heard that,' says Oti, walking out of their room. She is dressed as if for a theatrical fox hunt, in a full black skirt, ruffled shirt, a close-fitted red-velvet riding jacket and, perhaps as a nod to the poor, unfortunate fox, a small boxy hat trimmed with fur and a short black net veil. She looks magnificent. 'So, ladies, are you ready for our adventure?'

I nod, a fizz of anticipation in my tummy. Today could be the day we set Sally free.

'Let's go,' I say.

Oti pops a monocle in her eye as if it's the most normal thing in the world and off we go.

Clifton Lodge is perched high up on the far side of Brandon Hill, with views stretching towards the Avon. It's a handsome sight, its deep-yellow brickwork burnished by the autumn sun, so blended into its landscape that it, too, changes colour with the seasons.

The walk is almost entirely uphill, save the last little skip over the brow. We stop for a short rest next to the nearly completed Cabot Tower ('shame it isn't finished; you'd be able to see for *miiiiiles* from up there!' Cecily exclaims) but by the time we reach the Lodge my companions are quite out of puff, so we pause a moment against the dun-coloured bricks of the walled garden to the left of the driveway.

'I think you two should stay here while I go and knock,' I say, sounding more confident than I feel. On the way here I've told them about Sally and, although part of me would love to tell them *everything*, I keep in mind Pa's advice not to reveal the truth about my skill; they think I'm here to ask questions, nothing more. I can't have them earwigging, even if it means doing this alone.

Oti removes her monocle and peers at me. 'Are you sure? What if they don't let you in?'

Cecily hitches up her skirt and leans a foot against the wall. 'That's true,' she says, using her aristocratic accent again. 'In which case we may have traversed this wild landscape for nought.'

'It's taken us less than half an hour. And they have to let me in. They have to!' I am on the edge of tears, and they say nothing more.

It isn't until now that I realize I'm quite without a plan. To simply knock on the door and express my sympathies would not allow me the access I need to the house, and access is what I need if I'm to have any chance of making contact with the deceased Lady Stanton. But should entry be refused, or if her spirit has already moved on . . . what then?

I'm yet to fully understand it, any of it. The Sally I know will cry if she crunches a snail underfoot; she'll carry a spider from parlour to back yard sooner than squash it with a shoe. Sally is kind and sweet and trusting. Too trusting, at times. She's no killer, of that there can be no doubt; I can no more imagine it of her than of myself. *But then*, I think, *she does have a temper, and can be quick to react . . . No, no!* I push the thought away. Sally is innocent. And what of the other staff at the Lodge? Might they know what happened? Someone must know something, even if I can't find out the truth from Lady Stanton.

Emboldened, I walk up the drive towards the house. Four stone steps lead to a door with an elaborate knocker in the shape of a gargoyle.

I knock and wait.

And wait.

And wait.

Where *is* everyone? Frustrated, I push the door and gasp – it creaks open.

'Hello?' I whisper. 'Is anyone there?'

I step over the threshold, squinting into a gloomy, cavernous entrance hall, barely able to see my hand in front of my face. I pause, a trickle of dread creeping up my neck. There is movement up ahead in the gloom. I strain my eyes, trying to make sense out of the shape that is moving slowly but surely towards me.

'Lady Stanton?' I whisper, my voice hoarse and reluctant.

The shape moves closer, coal black, a slight glow at its middle casting long, confusing shadows. I can't fathom where it begins or ends.

'Oi!' says the shape angrily.

'S-sorry,' I stammer. 'I didn't know if anyone was at home. The door sort of . . . opened by itself.'

'Well, there's no one 'ome other than me, an' I'll not be thankin' you for 'angin' round 'ere. Be orf with ya!' On drawing closer, the shape shows itself to be a man in a black coat and cap, an old man, older than anyone I've ever seen not laid out in the dressing room back home.

'I'm sorry, sir,' I say. 'I've come to visit the mistress of the house.'

'The mistress isn't 'ere,' he replies. 'No one's 'ere. I thought I'd made that clear.'

'Sorry, yes, you did. Will she be back soon?' An idea comes to mind: 'I was told there may be . . . an opening 'ere for a lady's maid.'

At this, the old man stops. He has a large circle of keys in his hand and he rattles them at me, like an angry gaoler. 'What've you 'eard?' He leans in, close to my face. He smells of sour ale and manure.

'Nothing, nothing, I swear!'

He takes off his cap and holds it in his gnarled hand, nails thick with dirt. 'The lady of the 'ouse passed away recently, may God bless 'er soul,' he says, less angry now.

He's no taller than me, but his wiriness, his erratic temper and foul odour make me step back from him. I try to clear my mind to see if I can sense Lady Stanton, but all I hear is my lie growing bigger and my accent getting broader. 'I'm sorry to know that, sir. I was going round all the big 'ouses, sir, askin' about work, you see. Me daddy's lost his job and me ma says I've got to find employment or I'll be out on me backside. She told me to present meself at all the big 'ouses and ask, polite like, but not pushy, to see if one will take me on.'

He sucks in his cheeks, considering me and my story. 'Well,' he finally says, ''appen there might be a vacancy. They'll have to 'ire some new staff eventually.'

'If your mistress 'as passed,' I say innocently, 'is the 'ouse . . . being sold?'

At this, the old man's temper flares again. 'Well now, that's none of your business, you cheeky little beggar!' But, as before, he soon settles after the initial match-strike. 'You local?' he asks.

'From t'other side of the river.'

'Well,' he says, relaxing, 'I dare say there'll be a new master or mistress one day, but I can't tell you when that'll be. Once all the business 'as been sorted, then we'll see.' Suddenly his face crumples and to my horror tears fall unchecked down his goblin-like face.

'I . . . I'm terribly sorry,' I say. 'I didn't mean to upset you.'

He pulls a greying handkerchief from his pocket and blows his nose. 'Beggin' your pardon, miss. Not like me to show such emotion, but Lady Stanton was a diamond. Been with 'er for forty-odd years, me and most of the others. We were like a family.'

He trumpets into his handkerchief again and dabs at his rheumy eyes, barely visible within the dirt-etched folds of his face. 'I'm the gardener and the only staff at all at the minute. I'm 'ere to have a look round and lock the place up securely. I don't want no more trouble. T'ain't worth it.'

'Trouble?'

If he hears me, he doesn't acknowledge it. 'The gardens are beautiful,' I continue truthfully. 'There's surely an army of gardeners here, not just you.'

At this he unfurls like a rose. 'No, miss, it's just me. I'm the only one left.'

'Where's everyone else?'

'Gone,' he mutters, almost to himself. 'Lady Stanton said she'd see us right, but they all 'ad mouths to feed, and folks is funny about staying in a place after . . .'

My blood chills in my veins. 'After . . .?'

He looks up at me. 'Now you, that's enough chatter,' he says abruptly. 'Orf you go now and leave me to lock up.'

'Can I come back?' I ask. 'Maybe . . . after the funeral?'

'Funeral was yesterday, brought forward for some reason.' He sets his jaw. 'No chance for those that loved her to properly pay their respects neither. Private service and buried in the family crypt.'

'I'm sorry,' I say, and turn to go. Then something catches my eye, a glow in the deepest recess of the hall. An ember from the enormous fireplace perhaps? And wait . . . Is that . . . singing?

Yes. It's her. Lady Stanton's voice is thin and reedy, and not a little out of tune, but it's her.

I *must* stay in the house. But already the old man is edging me through the door, and before I know it we are on the steps outside and he's busying himself with the lock.

'I beg your pardon, sir, but could I use the facilities, please? Before I journey back home?'

He straightens and looks squarely at me. His head is level with the gargoyle doorknocker and the resemblance is uncanny. 'You speak quite proper for someone seekin' work in service,' he says accusingly.

'I . . . um –'

There is a sudden flurry and flap of tweed and velvet. 'Oh! Our hero! Thank heavens we caught you! . . . We feared for our very lives, but we are saved! . . . Come with us!' Cecily and Oti talk breathlessly, each grabbing an arm of the grumpy old gardener.

'Eh? What's goin' on?' he says, startled. He hasn't finished locking the door and I dive back through it. 'Oi,' he shouts, 'what you think ye're doin'?'

'I won't be a minute, I promise!'

'But –'

'Don't worry about her, my lovely.' Oti lifts her black-netted veil. 'Not when there's a, er, stranger lurking in the lupins!'

'Yes, that's it! A stranger. He gave us quite a start!' confirms Cecily.

'But she shouldn't be in the 'ouse by 'erself . . . an' what were you two doin' in my lupins?'

'Oh my, what an impertinent question to ask a lady!' Cecily trills, manoeuvring the old man towards the gardens and away from the house. Looking over her shoulder at me, she whispers, '*Go!*'

I step into the entrance hall, grand and panelled with great swathes of dark wood. Her spirit is here, but only just. 'Lady Stanton?' I say tentatively. 'Can I talk to you?'

Her voice is as wispy as early-morning mist and with each word she slides further away. I can barely make out anything she says. The speck of light glows brighter and brighter, piercing the darkness like a burning arrow until I have to look away.

'It isn't fair! It's not his! Get it back! Please, help me! Get it back! It's not his!'

And then she is gone.

She is gone.

It is as if someone has placed rocks in my pockets. I am weighted to the spot, hope draining out of me like water from a leaky bucket. I can't move, and where would I go even if I could? I'd placed so much hope in this visit; I'd hoped so much that Lady Stanton would help me save Sally.

She is gone.

My last remaining hope now is Sally. *If I can just talk to her in gaol* . . . It will all come down to that.

Noise from the girls outside snaps me out of my stupor and I step back towards the door, scrunching my eyes to focus them again. I notice some unopened letters on the hall table, and on one I recognize my own handwriting. My letter to Sally. Unread, unanswered.

Cecily, Oti and I walk back from the Lodge in silence. On our return a grim-faced Mr Bletchley tells me that my request to visit Sally has been refused, so where there was hope, now there is nothing at all.

15

My mood the past two days has been stormy, to say the least. Over and over I churn Lady Stanton's words – '*Get it back! It's not his!*' – hopeful that a lightning bolt of realization will strike and I'll understand what she means. But I am at a loss! I have no idea what to do now, or to whom I can turn next.

I asked Traitor Bletchley for help once more: could he use his influence, speak to someone senior at the gaol on Sally's behalf, perhaps? But no, he would not, lest it 'draw the wrong sort of attention' to the emporium. I raged at him in frustration, slamming the door so hard that when I opened it again seconds later his mouth still hung agape.

Astonishingly, there was but one person of whom I could think who might be able to help me, which no doubt came as much of a surprise to him as it did to me. And so it was that not an hour from then – heaven knows how I persuaded him so quickly – Mr Bletchley had readied his carriage for my use. 'I promised your mother I'd keep you out of mischief, Margaret, so no detours,' he said. 'Other than that, take all the time you need.'

I had told Mr Bletchley that it would help my mood to see a friendly face from home and so now here I am, sitting on a neat, black velvet sofa at the back of his funeral director's business in the middle of Bristol's Old Market. There are coffins everywhere. At least a dozen caskets border the interior of the showroom, silk-lined and polished, with shiny brass handles and elaborate, decorative inlays like wooden soldiers in dress uniforms. Each coffin is flagged by tree-sized black ostrich plumes, and a battalion of headstones stands to attention in one corner. In spite of the decor, I like it here; at least now that I am inside and sipping a cup of hot, sweet tea.

The city is overwhelming; it is entirely *full*, in a way that was previously unimaginable to me, coming from the countryside. There are buildings everywhere, in every space, of every style: black-and-white half-timbered Tudor houses nestled among modern red brick or classical Bath stone facades, and where there is not a building there is a tram, or a planted pot, or a bench, or a drinking fountain, or a monument. The driver pointed out the newest addition, a statue of a pompous-looking sort of man, in a powdered wig and breeches. Even the dolphins that flank him seemed to have one eye on the water beyond – and who wouldn't, stuck with a fellow such as he? Perhaps someday they will have their freedom, one way or another.

The city is also full of spirits, dotted throughout the crowded streets. I see one – my eyes adjust and I see there's another, and another. A man in a top hat, knife protruding from his back; a woman pushing a pram, dripping with water and laced with weeds from the river; three small children, faces burning with pox, and countless others with no outward signs of how they met their demise. Why some are cast in their moment of death, and some are not, I have no idea. There is no obvious glow surrounding them, as with those I typically see on their burn. In fact, I could have easily overlooked them from my position in the carriage, were it not for the fact that each one very slowly turned their head to look at me as I passed. Has it always been so? Countless dead eyes, staring at me?

I shake away the images, coming back to myself, and blow the steam from my cup. Across from me sits Ambrose, who is in charge of the office in the manager's absence.

'No one in today, Peggy. Can you ... feel anything?' he asks, fiddling with the catalogues of funeral paraphernalia fanned out on the table between us. I pause for a moment. Nothing. It is entirely soulless in here. I shake my head and Ambrose's shoulders drop by a good few inches. All pretence has now gone – he knows what I am, always has, but now it is part of our shared truth.

'I hate coming here,' he confesses, 'even when the manager's in.' He shudders. 'Not that I'd admit it and risk my apprenticeship. Father would be fuming, for a start. I'd never seen him proud of me before Jed –' he colours – 'before Mr Bletchley sought me out.'

'What do you mean, he sought you out?'

'Mr Bletchley said he'd heard through mutual friends that I'd make a fine apprentice to the establishment. Who these mutual friends are neither Father nor I could fathom, but no matter.' He smiles. 'Perhaps I'll learn to love it.'

'Oh, Ambrose, I'm not going to feel sorry for you and your effortlessly won career. Leave if you don't like it. I doubt you'll be destitute – your father is a wealthy man; he'd hardly let you starve.'

'I wouldn't be so sure. I sometimes think Father regrets his one charitable act, or at least wishes he'd picked a different orphan to adopt. He must realize by now that it's unlikely any future generations of Shipwell will come from me,' he says ruefully.

I've always known that Ambrose likes boys more than girls, ever since he said that one of the lads from the farm made his tummy feel fizzy. I never thought anyone would think less of him for it, especially not his own pa. I'd lean over and give him a hug, but there really isn't time.

'Ambrose, I'm in a bit of a bind,' I say, and fill him in on the events at Clifton Lodge. He nods, thoughtfully, eyes widening when I get to the part about Lady Stanton's ghost and her mysterious message. I slump on the sofa and brush biscuit crumbs from my dress. 'I don't know what to do,' I say forlornly. 'If I could speak to Sally, then maybe she *might* give me a clue about what I should do next, but she's stuck in that awful gaol and I can't get to her at all! Mr Bletchley won't help me. Can you think of anything?'

Ambrose shakes his head, eyes flicking between me and the coffins, no doubt unsettled by my talk of spirits. As I regard him, I feel the *tick tick tick* of a plan forming in my mind.

'You're his assistant, aren't you?' I ask.

'What?'

'You, Ambrose. You're Bletchley's assistant.'

'Ye-e-s?' He eyes me suspiciously. 'Spit it out, Peg. What do you want?'

'Do you think *you* could do it somehow? Get a message to Sally at the gaol for me?'

Ambrose shrugs, brow furrowing behind the angelic curls of his fringe. 'I don't know, Peggy. I occasionally have to go up there for work, but not often. I'm not sure how much clout I have, even as Jed's assistant . . . but I will try, on that you have my word.'

He looks so earnest my stomach twists and I want to hug him again. 'I know you will. Thank you, Ambrose.'

'You know, I can't believe it of her – Sally, I mean – scrappy little thing that she is. You recall when she made us break into the chemist's?'

'It was hardly breaking in, more of a snoop round outside, but, gosh – yes! And we went along with it!'

Ambrose laughs. 'I was far more scared of Sally's temper than of Mrs Dulwich, even though I was terrified Mrs Dulwich would find us and turn us all into toads!'

'Oh, Ambrose! She's a harmless old lady.'

He cocks his head to one side, like a dog.

'Well, all right, maybe not harmless,' I concede, 'but she's no witch. I don't think Sally believed she was, either, not that Sally would have been troubled by it. That sort of stuff doesn't bother her.' I shrug a half-apology at Ambrose, suddenly regretful that I wasn't brave enough to share my secret with him before now. 'It was larks, that was all. You know what she's like,' I say. 'Always the first to jump into the weir, always the first to talk to a newcomer in the village, always the first up to dance. She throws herself headlong into everything. She always wants to *do* stuff, to *know* stuff.'

'To live life to the full,' Ambrose puts in.

'Yes. Exactly that.' I feel the spiky prickle of tears and swallow them back. 'I keep thinking of her, Ambrose, in there all alone. I pray her family have been able to see her.'

'I think not,' he says. 'Apparently she's to see no one. Too distressing for her.'

'On whose say-so? Mr Bletchley's?'

'Why on earth would it be him? Even if you were correct to mistrust him, Peggy, which I really don't think you are, he has no authority at the gaol. How would he even engineer such a thing?'

I pause at this. Ambrose is quite right, of course. Mr Bletchley is up to something, though, and I'm determined to find out what. And if it isn't Bletchley, then *someone* is trying to thwart Sally's freedom, but who, and why?

Ambrose promised to do his very best to deliver the note I hastily wrote to Sally on a sheet of black-edged stationery before Mr Bletchley's driver called me to leave. All I can do is wait for word from Ambrose, or for Sally to reply, if she possibly can. Wait, and intercept the post each day as it drops through the letterbox on to the marble floor in the hall, in case whoever seeks to sabotage my plan is waiting for the postman, too. As a result, I am quite exhausted, and not a little homesick. This morning I dash to the door as usual as the letters drop through and, disheartened at not finding word for me, start making my way back to my room, when . . .

Crrrang-crrrang! Crrrang-crrrang!

My heart leaps up to my throat – what is that terrible racket? I don't immediately recognize the sound, or understand where the shrill clatter can be coming from, but then I realize it's the telephone.

Gingerly I make my way to the brown box on the wall. Such a small thing making such a horrendous, enormous noise! Should I answer it?

Crrrang-crrrang!

I pick up the receiver and hold it to my ear, as Mr Bletchley demonstrated when he'd explained the contraption to me. 'Um, yes?' I say into the mouthpiece. The line crackles and spits like bacon in a pan and I am about to hang up and run when I hear, 'Peggy? Peggy, is that you?'

Warmth washes over me like custard on to a crumble. 'Mama?'

'Peggy? Oh, Peggy! My love, I've been so worried!'

'Oh, Mama! I miss you so! And Wolf, and Pa of course!'

'I've so much to tell you!' we say in unison.

'You go first,' Mama says, 'but speak quickly; I'm in the manager's office at the mine. It's the only place in Alderley with one of these things. I'm not sure how long I've got and it must be costing a fortune.'

'Oh, Mama! I don't know where to start! I don't know who to trust and I tried to speak to Lady Stanton but that was no use and I'm not sure what Mr Bletchley is about and –'

Click . . . click . . . hssshh . . . hssshh.

'What was that?'

'I don't know,' says Mama slowly. 'It sounds like . . . breathing. We should be careful what we say, Peg, I'm not too sure I trust these new-fangled machines. But, just so you know, I'm doing everything I can here. I call in to see the Hubbards most days, and they're being so brave, and yesterday Annie said that Mr Hubbard hadn't had a drink for *hours*, which is a miracle. I'm trying everything.'

I slump against the wall. 'I don't know what more I can do here, Mama. I have no solution. I feel all may be lost.'

'I see.'

'And everything's strange here and the air smells different and I miss you so, and Wolf, and I want to come home!'

'No.'

No? I stare at the wall in front of me incredulously, as if expecting to see Mama's face on it. 'But . . .'

'No buts!' she says crisply. 'There's always a way. You just haven't found it yet. I know I didn't want you to go to Bristol to start with, but I trust you, Peggy. You are not to give up, you hear me? Is there anyone there you can talk to? Apart from Jedediah?'

'*Pfft!* As if I'd talk to *him*.'

'You can't always do everything on your own, Peggy.'

'But I *should* be able to do more than this! I should! But I can't. I'm hopeless.'

'You are *not* hopeless. You are Peggy Devona and you are my daughter. My wonderful, brave daughter.' There's a slight catch in her voice and I force back tears. 'Have patience, Peggy. Keep banging on doors – that's what I'm going to carry on doing here. All we can do is pray that sooner or later one will open.'

You can't always do everything on your own, Peggy . . . Keep banging on doors . . . sooner or later one will open. I'm drifting again, in and out of sleep. I dream of Sally and Ambrose, of telephones that speak to me with voices of the dead, of my bleeding fists pounding on door after door after unanswered door –

Crack!

A snap of energy yanks me awake. My scalp tingles.

'*Together.*'

I peek out from under the covers and my blood chills in my veins.

She's here.

Sputtering in and out of focus is the flickering, unsettling ghost girl from home. She is here, in my little Bristol attic room, twitching like a divining willow in the corner next to the washstand. She's holding something, clutching it to her like a baby.

'What do you want?' My voice shakes. 'Who are you? Why are you following me?' I pause. '*How* are you following me? Ghosts can't follow people, can they?'

She stills, briefly, and I catch her expression. It is exactly mine when Mama asks if I'll ever get round to tidying my bedroom. And then she shrugs.

I've never seen a ghost *shrug* either.

I have got this very, very wrong. She's not here to frighten me. Could she be here to help?

I push off the bedcovers and scrabble towards her on all fours until I'm kneeling at the end of the bed. 'What is it?' I ask her. 'What are you trying to tell me?'

She squints, mouthing something I can't make out. 'What is it?' I say. 'Please, tell me! Please!'

'*Together*,' she repeats, but already she is puttering out, bleaching into the putty-coloured wall as we reach for each other, fingertips almost touching as she carousels away.

I sit for a while, willing her to return, but the room has settled.

Who is *she?* I wonder. And why . . . *how* . . . does this girl, this spirit girl that acts like no other spirit I have ever seen . . . how does she have the Book of Devona?

After a fitful sleep, I stumble downstairs and almost slam straight into Dotty.

'Watch where ye're goin'!' she shrieks, stretching her neck to yell at me over a tray laden with dirty plates up to her chin. I flush, embarrassed to be so preoccupied with ghost girls and ancient books that I didn't even see her. Her skinny knees buckle and as she topples backwards I just manage to grab a couple of slimy, fish-smeared plates before they skid to the floor.

She eyes me suspiciously.

'Here, let me help.' I wrinkle my nose. There is a distinct hum of haddock. 'That smells.'

'Well, ain't you the observant one,' she snaps huffily as I follow her slightly rocky, bow-legged walk to the kitchen. Rickets, most likely. Mama says everyone's got it in the city on account of the wrong sort of sunlight. Little wonder she's prickly towards me, for I am another mouth to feed and body to clear up after.

I insist on helping to wash up, for she was carrying more crockery on that tray than we've got at home (and that includes the good china), and slowly her features soften and she looks like the young girl she is. She tells me of her family, how she is one of seven; how her father goes looking for work each dawn at the docks, waiting alongside hundreds of others, and how with each passing year there are more men there that are fitter and faster and more likely to be picked for labour before him. I tell her a version of my life, less complicated than the truth, and as we walk through the house I believe us to be now companionable. But as we walk by Cecily and Oti's door, her face pinches up as if she's remembering she should be angry with me.

She nods towards the girls' room. 'Hang on,' she says warily, 'I thought you were s'posed to be helpin' those two, least that's what I heard.' She sidles up like a fox to an unsuspecting chicken and for a moment I think she may actually sniff me. 'Was that the *business* you meant when you arrived? Or is there another reason you're here?'

I move back a step. Where has she heard all this? Who's been talking about me? 'You're right,' I say. 'I'm here to help out at the emporium.'

'So why didn't you say so when you first got here, when I was tellin' you about all the weird stuff what goes on in that room? Bit rude.'

'Um, yes, sorry. I should have said; I just wasn't sure –'

'I shouldn't have said nothin', don't mind me. All a bit of harmless fun, innit?' She fixes me with a look. 'Unless you happen to be a creeper or summut.' She peers closer and I can smell sour milk on her breath. 'An' you ain't one of them, are you?'

I freeze, thoroughly wrong-footed, and then notice Mrs Morris pottering around in the emporium's waiting area. Her broad hips nudge the ebony cabinet and the impact wobbles a tiny shrunken head from its stand, causing it to fall with a *clonk*.

Dotty jumps and pales. 'Gotta go,' she says, already scurrying back towards the kitchen, clutching her mob cap to her head as she zips away.

Mrs Morris, too, has gone and I remain alone on the landing, baffled by Dotty's conflicting behaviour.

I think of Mama's words, of what the ghost girl said, and of Sally. And suddenly I know what I'm to do. Everything has been leading me here. Then, remembering Sally's way of plunging straight into things, I walk up to Oti and Cecily's door and knock.

18

Seven hours later, I am under a table in a small, dark box, waiting for my prompt.

The room is as murky as a mausoleum, the only light coming from a scattering of candles round the perimeter of the room, while bowls of sweet-smelling unction give off a heady aroma. Crystal balls and strange, unsettling objects (a stuffed fox with a waxen, human face I swear watches me) dress the room, reminding our guests that nothing here is normal. *This is mystical*, the room says. *This is other-worldly. You won't understand it, so don't question it.*

Cecily's voice is cool and hypnotic. 'Feeeel the energy flowing through you,' she drawls, 'through your fingers, through your body. Keep your hands linked together.'

'Why *is* that, Miss Richmond?' asks the troublesome man to her left, a Mr Grady. He has been fidgety since he arrived less than twenty minutes ago. It did not start well for him, this experience, mistaking Oti as he did for a parlour maid. He wordlessly handed her his greatcoat, which she dropped to the floor, stepping over it with a terse *No*.

The fool. How many parlour maids has he seen dressed as Oti is this evening? She wears a full-skirted, bronze satin gown and a fringed black velvet shawl that drips over her shoulders like treacle. She is a queen, not a parlour maid.

'My dear Mr Grady,' replies Cecily with the patience of a governess talking to her most simple charge when their mother is watching, 'the spirits react to the flow of energy between those in the circle. If the circle isn't complete, the energy isn't contained and is therefore useless. It's physics really.'

'Physics, you say?' His tone suggests a sceptically raised eyebrow, and I imagine Mrs Grady ignoring it, her lips a thin, dry line of disapproval.

'Do be quiet, Algernon,' she snipes. 'You are interrupting my experience. Do you have any idea how lucky we are to have even got an invitation?'

'Well, you didn't have to drag me along,' he grumbles.

'Oh, do stop bellyaching, Algie!'

A terse cough from Oti. 'The flow of energy round the circle, if complete, can be as strong as any chain. It binds those who believe in its power together, with as much of an iron grip as a chain holds those in a chain gang.' She pauses. 'But I forget – *you're* the expert on that, Mr Grady. Isn't that how you like to shackle workers on your plantation, chained together at the ankle and wrist and dragged for miles like livestock?' I can't see her face, but I can imagine Oti giving him the sweetest of smiles. 'And how *is* business at the plantation, Mr Grady?'

'Fine, fine,' he mutters.

'Perhaps there'll be a statue in your honour one day, like the one they've put up of Mr Colston. Wouldn't *that* be fitting?'

Colston. That was who it was for, the statue with the dolphins – that's the one I saw the other day.

I can feel Mr Grady's discomfort from underneath the table.

'Can you hear me, O dear spirits?' Cecily continues. 'O departed souls, perished beings that once walked among us, are you there?' She lowers her voice to a husky whisper, so the crackle of the fire can still be heard. Her dress this evening is like a ballet dancer's gown: wispy, sheer chiffon over a silky bodice, and flowing tulle skirts that rustle and billow, cloud-like, when she moves.

'Is she here? Will she make herself known?' Mrs Grady is persistent. 'Oh, this is so terribly exciting! Wait until I see the ladies at bridge club on Tuesday! They'll be positively green with –'

'Quiet, woman,' Oti snaps, and it makes me smile to think of the affronted look on Mrs Grady's face. Mama would love Oti.

'Ottoline, that's no way to talk to our esteemed guests,' chides Cecily. 'But she is right, Mrs Grady – allow the process to happen; it can't be forced. Now, everyone, be silent and use your mind's eye to show your strongest memory of – ' she pauses; I guess that she's glancing down at her leg where a reminder of the cast list is pinned between the folds of her skirts – 'Mother Beresford.'

Mrs Grady dares a whisper. 'Mama-bee, that's what I called her.' She sniffs. There is a pause and I picture her dabbing at her eye with a lace handkerchief. 'Dear, sweet Mama-bee.'

The room falls silent, save for the crackle of the fire, the swish of Oti's gown as she circles the table wafting incense like a smoking lioness, and the shallow, dry-eyed sobs of Mrs Grady. A low moan comes from Cecily.

This is my cue.

There are two small holes drilled on each side of the box for me to look through and through which I can breathe. There is also a narrow slot, halfway down one side, just wide enough for me to get my hand through.

I have 'equipment' – a stick with a feather tied to one end and a small brass doorknob screwed to the other, a drinking straw, a small bottle of perfume, a handful of rose petals, and a tiny package tied with string, which I tuck into my pinafore pocket. On Cecily's moan, which she lengthens to cover up any shuffling, I dip the drinking straw into the perfume bottle ('*Do* not *suck it in* – it's powerful stuff and I can't be certain it won't kill you!'), lean down to the narrow slot and blow. Drops of perfume sprinkle in the direction of Mrs Grady's skirts. Cecily was right; it is horribly pungent and the cloying rose scent sticks in my throat and pricks at my eyes.

'Mama-bee, are you here with us?' Cecily calls. 'Can you show us a sign?' At this, I push the stick, knob end first, through the slot and tap, once, on the floor.

Thud.

'Oh! What was that?'

'Did you hear something?'

'Where did it come from?'

'Was it from over here?' A shuffling of a chair.

'Do *not* break the chain,' orders Oti, and the shuffling stills.

Thud.

'There! I heard it again, I heard it again! Mother, Mama-bee – is that you?'

Thud. Thud.

'Mama-bee? Oh, Algernon, I think it's her . . . I can smell . . . roses!'

'Then ask her, Marian, ask her.'

'Don't be ridiculous! I can't ask her immediately. For heaven's sake, Algie, where are your manners?'

'Sorry, Marian dear.'

In the kerfuffle, I've slipped out of the box, which is hinged at the back, and, with the stick tucked under my arm, I crawl towards the only marker I have – a tiny, barely glowing oil lamp at the side of

Oti's chair. Her chair is narrower than the others, and set at an angle, so I can slip out unnoticed. The tang of incense is stronger over here and as I crawl round the table I'm disorientated – am I going the right way?

'I feel her coming through,' Cecily calls out in an eerie voice. 'She is next to you, Mrs Grady, warming herself *close by the fire* – as she did in life, did she not?'

I grimace at the astounded mutterings that ripple round the table, but I change route and head towards the grate, grateful for Cecily's direction. For as much as I know this to be manipulative trickery, I don't want to mess it up. These girls are helping me, so I will help them.

The aroma of rose wafting from Mrs Grady's skirts tells me I'm almost there and I move round so I'm in position between her and Cecily. I take my stick and stretch out my arm, stroking Mrs Grady's ankle with the feather end.

'What on earth was that!' she shrieks, jumping in her chair.

'Do *not* break the chain,' thunders Oti. 'You must stay still! You are feeling the touch of your loved one. Relax. Be calm – and don't keep jumping about.'

'Yes, of course. I'm so terribly sorry.'

I can just about see Oti on the other side of the table, sitting sideways on her chair, one leg dangling languidly over an arm. She is quite the distraction. Both of the girls are, in fact, which I suppose is the idea.

Cecily leans over to her right, her lips almost grazing the woman's ear. 'Yes, Mrs Grady, relax; close your eyes,' she murmurs. 'She is with us. This is a very special moment. Release yourself into it; let yourself go.' She waits, her face so close to Mrs Grady's that surely the lady must feel the whisper of Cecily's breath against her skin.

Careful to stay out of the Gradys' view, I stretch upwards and gently stroke the feather behind Mrs Grady's ears, down the nape of her neck. It's having a hypnotic effect on her. 'Mama-bee?' she whispers.

'Ask her, my dear,' says Mr Grady once more.

'Very well,' says Mrs Grady, sounding almost drunk. This room has that sort of effect on you, being so dark and womb-like, with its heady mix of cloying incense, the rose essence and heat from the fire.

Mrs Grady swallows, her head lolling gently from side to side. 'Mama-bee, my darling, I must ask you a question. May I?'

'One knock for yes, two for no,' says Cecily, by way of a reminder to me. I slide back until I reach the skirting board and tuck myself away behind the heavy velvet curtains. I knock once with the brass end of my stick. The sound of the knock reverberates around the room, the deep skirting boards acting like a sound box to send it echoing from wall to wall.

'That's *yes!*' the deluded Mrs Grady gasps.

'Please, continue, Mrs Grady,' urges Cecily. 'The spirits are receptive tonight.'

'Mama-bee, I miss you so greatly – we all do . . . don't we, Algie?'

'Yes, dear, that we do.'

'Darling Mama-bee, I have a question about your will. I know you were always so very charitably minded, but did you really intend to leave quite so much to the municipal children's home?'

I can't see Mrs Grady, but the sour expression is obvious. I thump the skirting board once, hard. How dare she?

'Was that yes, Mama-bee? You did intend to leave them that amount of money?' Her voice is unnaturally high now and quavering, full of greedy hope.

Thud goes my stick.

'But you know we were hoping to move to a larger property after you die . . . after . . . well, we stayed so you could be close to your good causes and philanthropic societies, but now we'd like to move out of town – perhaps it would help us deal with your demise not to stay in the family home, and we promised Lucy a pony – she's so disappointed – so would you mind perhaps if I . . . perhaps . . . contested the will?'

Thud.

'Oh.'

Thud.

'What? Does that mean no? You wouldn't mind? She wouldn't mind, Algie!'

Thud. Thud. Thud. Thud. Thud thud thud thud thud thud thud thud thud thud thud.

'Oh my, whatever does that mean? I've upset her. I'm sorry, Mama-bee, I'm sorry!'

BANG! Flames roar into the room from the fireplace, whooshing and crackling furiously before reeling back like angry, blazing waves in the stormy seas of Hell.

'Aaargh! The fire – it's alive! The fire!'

'Get back, get back!'

'Oh mercy, what on earth is happening?'

'It's Mother Beresford! We've angered her!'

The flash and growl from the fire is brutal, even from behind the curtain, and the screams from the Gradys (and the girls, who shriek with gusto) are disorientating and frightening. My heart is pounding in my chest so hard I swear it may split my ribs and fly right out of me. I throw my final prop from underneath the curtain, praying it hits its mark.

'It's all right, everyone, it's all right.' Cecily's voice is calming and soft, her gentle tone a balm to the spiky atmosphere. 'Sometimes the spirits find new ways of letting us know their feelings. Do you feel that you have your message, Mrs Grady?'

I almost giggle out loud.

'Well, yes, assuming it was indeed Mama-bee . . . Of course, one can't be sure . . .'

'Marian,' says Algie suddenly, 'what's that on your gown?'

'What do you mean, Algernon dear? Where? Oh! Oh, Algernon! It's rose petals! Rose petals, Algie! Oh, Mama-bee, it really *is* you! I'm so sorry – I should never have asked. Of course those poor children should have the money, of course they should. Please forgive me, Mama-bee. I'll never question your wishes again.'

'Did you see her face when the fire exploded? It was incredible! Oh my gosh, we should've materialized something at that point – they would've believed anything!' Cecily is glowing, her face sheeny with triumph and gin.

'I know!' Oti hands Cecily another full glass. 'I thought Mrs Grady was going to self-combust. Even old Algernon looked like he'd actually seen a ghost!'

'You were brilliant, darling Margaret! The timing was spot on. You threw that firecracker with such fabulous accuracy! Perhaps you should try your hand at cricket. Do you play?'

I shake my head.

'Shame,' says Cecily. 'You'd make a most excellent bowler.'

I sit on a chair in the corner of the now tidied room. The windows have been thrown open to rid it of fumes from incense and gunpowder (the latter from my well-thrown firecracker), candles have been doused, lamps lit and detritus tidied away so that, on first examination, it looks like a perfectly respectable parlour again. The girls have changed into full-length smoking jackets, monogrammed with 'CR' and 'OA' respectively.

'What does the A stand for?' I ask, adding before I can stop myself: 'Apart from *actress* . . .'

'Aseema. Ottoline Aseema, at your service, Lady Margaret.' Oti affects an exaggerated bow and flourish. 'Something wrong, little one?'

Her theatricality makes me feel uneasy, but I find it hard to look away from her; she is so striking.

'Sorry, Oti, I didn't mean to sound so snippy.'

'Are you sure? Ceci, I think our protégée has something to say.'

'Oh? What is it, Margaret?' Cecily sets down her glass, walks over and crouches next to me. 'What's the matter?'

'I don't know really,' I begin shyly. 'I mean, it was . . . exciting. I wasn't expecting that. And those greedy people, trying to grab money away from a children's home of all things; well, they certainly deserved scaring . . . but . . .' I pause, not wanting to give offence. 'Doesn't it seem wrong to you, making people think they're communicating with dead relatives when all the time it's a conjuring trick designed to fleece them of their money?'

'A guinea isn't exactly a lot of money to the people that come here,' Cecily retorts. 'No one is invited who can't afford it − that would be unethical.'

'And our guests were very happy when they left, weren't they?' Oti adds. 'They could barely keep their faces straight for the photograph! You must have heard them, Peggy?'

It's true. There had been much laughter when the Gradys left the parlour; even the *boof* of the camera flash caused shrieks of nervous hilarity. 'I know, and that's why I feel so −'

'Judgemental?' Cecily looks at me intently, cornflower-blue eyes sparking with devilment.

I grin. She's right: I *am* being judgemental.

'I was going to say *torn*,' I say. 'But they were terrible people, so I don't feel so bad about tricking them.'

'Tricking them?' Cecily holds a hand to her chest in mock horror. 'How could you say such a thing!' She pirouettes around the room, grabs Oti by the hand and drags her to the table.

'Stop it, you mad woman!' Oti laughs. 'What are you doing?'

'I want to show our doubting assistant that we're very much the real thing!' Cecily throws her head back and closes her eyes, gripping Oti's hands tightly. 'Is anybody there?' she says in a booming baritone. She opens one eye to peep at me. 'Quick, little ghost! Fly over here and poke Oti in the nose with your feathery spirit stick!'

'Ceci, no, stop it! What if Mr Bletchley hears? He won't take kindly to the mockery – you know what he's like,' says Oti gravely, scrunching her features as a handful of rose petals are blown in her face. 'Ceci, stop!'

'Oh, pish-posh, don't be such a stuffy-pants.' Cecily pouts tipsily, but then she winks at me. 'I'm jus' muckin' about! I know it's all rubbish, like I told Bletchy-chops after he saw us at that music hall. But no, no – he insisted on us comin' to work for him. Well, I say "us" – it was Oti he wanted, but we come as a pair, don't we, bab?'

'He's been very good to us, Ceci – you know that,' said Oti. 'And after he closed down his other psychic emporiums, we're lucky to still have a job.'

'What do you mean, his "other psychic emporiums"?' I say, walking over to the table and pulling up a chair.

'It's nothing to worry about, truly. Forget we said anything.' Cecily leans over the table and places a hand over my wrist to reassure me.

'I . . . I'm not worried.' I look from Oti to Cecily and back again. '*Should* I be worried, Oti?'

'Mr Bletchley had some psychic emporiums abroad,' she replies. 'But he received a few threats overseas. Seems that not everyone is keen on spiritualism, real or fake or otherwise. But it's nothing to worry about – we're perfectly safe here.'

'Which is just as well, as we have nowhere else to go,' says Cecily into her gin glass.

Oti smiles and rolls her eyes. 'Really, it's nothing to worry about, poppet.' She clasps my other hand so the three of us are linked. 'Ouch! What the –?' she gasps.

She feels it – we all feel it: the electric crackle in our fingers like static from a hundred hairbrushes.

I try to release my hand, knowing what is to come, but it's too late; the breath is knocked from my lungs like a punch to my chest.

'*Oof!*' I cry from pain and fear as the air in the room shifts and separates, making way.

'What's happening?' says Oti, ducking down. 'Oh my saints and sinners, what *are* they?'

She can see them too? These iridescent, ancient things that whoosh and spin like leaves on the breeze, gossamer light, rushing and whirling like ribbons caught in a cyclone, the speed of them unworldly and unsettling. Occasionally, they twist and form, layer over gauzy layer, into the people they once were before they lifted away from their bodies.

They really are everywhere.

I've known this truth since I read it in the Book of Devona, before Pa snatched it away, but I've never seen them like this before. There are new spirits on their burn; there are old spirits that either return or don't manage to leave, for whatever reason – and then there is this. This *energy*. Good and evil, ancient and new, caught between here and there. *What did it say, the rest of the passage, about how to enter the realm?*

And how, more importantly, to leave it?

'Fill your head!' I shout, remembering what Pa had said. 'Fill your head with thoughts so they can't get in!'

'How do you know all this? How do you know?' Cecily has her head on the table, eyes tight shut. 'Is it a trick? Please let it be a trick.' She's crying. 'It can't be real, this isn't real, we're not really psychic, we've been tested! Margaret . . . Peggy – tell them. We'll not do it again, will we? We were only playing, weren't we? Oti and I are fakes, they must know that! We can't really talk to spirits, we aren't real whisperlings!'

'I know you aren't, Cecily. But I am. I am.'

I'm surrounded now, drowning in the swirling energy, faces coming at me from the storm like fragments of flotsam from a churning phantom sea. The whole room crackles with terrible energy, entities filling every space, saturating every inch.

Whatever barrier separates their realm from ours is as fragile as a soap bubble.

A vase topples from the mantelpiece and smashes on the hearth, a painting flies from the wall, velvet curtains rip like tissue paper, books are tossed into the fire that spits and roars with rage. Something tears at my arms and legs and I cry out as angry red welts appear from nowhere on my skin.

I can't hold on.

I scream as a scalding poker hits my wrist – *Who did that?* – and I release my grip. As the smell of burning flesh hits my throat I fall to the floor, and all there is, is the dark.

One day, when I was around ten and she twelve, Sally and I took a walk to St Mary's Church at the top of Bothwick Hill. Confetti fluttered around the gravestones from a wedding that had taken place earlier, tiny scraps of paper lifted and spun by a brisk spring breeze. We ran after them like kittens chasing butterflies, gathering handfuls to throw in the air for our own pretend wedding.

Out of puff, we stopped for a breather. Sally's hair, red as a sunset and coiled into a loose bun, was scattered with confetti jewels.

'You reckon,' she said, pulling the stopper from a bottle of homemade lemonade with her teeth, 'if you stood here nice an' quiet like, you could hear anything from – ' she nodded her head to the raised hump of ground beneath her feet – 'down there?'

'Get off it, Sal – it's disrespectful,' I said, giving her a shove.

She stumbled theatrically and fell to the floor in a giggling heap. She winked at me, took a swig from the bottle and lay down on the grass with her head on the grave like it was a grassy pillow.

'Is there anybody *therrrrrre*?' she whispered, wrinkling her nose at the tickling grass.

'Stop it, you gommo.'

But a moment later I'm there, right by her, and we lie as still as those beneath us, listening. There was nothing, though, just the sound of the murmuring breeze.

'Don't look so disappointed,' she said, affectionately poking the end of my nose with her finger. 'I was only messin'. But if you want to try again, we can.'

'There's no point,' I say. 'It doesn't work like that.'

'How do you know? You're only a beginner, an' you're better at this stuff than anyone in the world, far as we know.'

I shrug.

'Look at me an' my readin'!' she reminds me. 'Never thought I'd be able to do that, did I? Don't give up, Peg.'

It makes me ashamed to admit it, but giving up is all I want to do.

It has been a day and a half since the seance, and I have not spoken to anyone since the wound on my wrist was dressed by a shaken Cecily. I can't. I just can't. I sink my head into my hands as I hear footsteps thud up the stairs – I don't want to see *anyone*; they can *go away*. The door flies open and Oti marches in. She wears plum silk pyjamas nipped in with a wide, knotted belt at the waist and cream buttoned boots trimmed with lace.

'I have come to take you back into civilization,' she announces, the ropes of pearls wrapped round her wrist clattering as she waggles a finger at me. 'You can't hide in here, little one, we must –' She sees my packed bag and glares from me to it and back again and I shrink into the bed. 'What's this?' Oti's voice is sharp. '*You're leaving?*'

She aims a kick at my carpet bag, sending it skidding towards me, her voluminous trousers rippling with the action. My journal, balancing on top, lands at Oti's feet and she picks it up, turning it over in her hands. I grab it from her and retreat back to my bed, where I sit cross-legged, stroking the blue cover as if it were an animal.

'You are *not* running away!' Oti commands. 'Not on my watch. We have to talk about what happened, Peggy.'

'No.'

'What *was* it?'

'I don't know.'

'Yes, you do!' she persists. 'You told us what to do! You said you were a whisperling!'

'I can't, Oti! I promised Pa –'

'Your pa isn't here. And this happened to us too. It isn't just about you any more. And what about Sally? Mr Bletchley –'

'What?' My head snaps up. 'What did he say?'

'He said that he is your uncle. That it was your truth to tell. He knows, doesn't he? Is that why he kept testing me, to see if I was one too? Peggy, please talk to me! I'm frightened!'

There is a gentle knock at the door. 'May I come in?' asks Cecily.

'Of course,' I croak. 'Thank you for asking,' and I throw a pointed look at Oti, who ignores me.

'Margaret? Oti?' Cecily says tentatively. 'Is everything all right? What are you . . . oh –' She notices my packed bag, and then my face, red and puffy from crying and lack of sleep. She glares at Oti. 'Did you make her cry?'

'No! I did not make her cry. She was already crying.'

'Have you comforted her?'

'No, not yet,' Oti replies. 'I was too annoyed that she was leaving. I'll get round to it in a moment.'

Cecily tuts, pulling her skirts round her and bunching them between her legs. She eases herself on to the bed as if sitting side-saddle on a horse and places a soft, cool hand over mine. There is the slightest shimmer of residual energy between Cecily's hand and mine, not like before but there nonetheless. 'Right then, babber. Why do you want to leave?'

'I can't help Sally. I don't know what to do,' I admit. 'And then . . . *that* happened.'

'Ah. You're leggin' it. Runnin' away. I see.'

'No! I mean . . . yes. Oh, I don't know!'

'And you're sure that Sally is innocent?'

'Yes!' I snap. 'Of course she is!'

Cecily nods. 'So, what shall we do about it?'

I sink into my pillow. 'I don't know! I tried to speak to Lady Stanton and couldn't. Then I tried to get a message to Sally and failed at that as well. If I could just get someone, anyone who is in charge, to listen, get them into a room somehow . . . but I can't do it on my own!'

'But you're not on your own, are you? You have us. And we are excellent.' Cecily taps me on the top of my head and I smile weakly. 'But if we're to help . . .'

They both look at me, waiting.

I'm sorry, Pa. Sometimes you shouldn't *keep your trap shut.* I take a breath, and make the leap.

'So, tell me again?' says Cecily, brow furrowed in concentration. I feel like I'm back in the school-room with Mama. *Oh Mama!* And the children. The empty seat where Bertie should be . . . The emotion punches me hard in the stomach but I shove it away.

'When someone dies, their spirit is at its strongest,' I begin. 'If it's going to be seen by anyone – someone close to them, or someone like me – it will be then, at the moment of their death. We call it the burn. With the Devonas, it's only the women in the family who have the gift to speak with spirits, and in some generations the gift isn't that strong at all. I don't know if it's the same for other whisperlings.' I shrug. 'Having not met any.'

Oti sits on the floor, cross-legged with one arm wound round Cecily's leg, which dangles off my bed. 'And how long does this *burn* last for?' she asks.

'It depends. Sometimes it's minutes, sometimes hours.' I hesitate. 'Sometimes much longer.'

'Where do they go, after that?' says Cecily.

'I don't know. But they go somewhere – at least, most of them do, and the majority stay there. It's only those that are unsettled who come back. Or those that want to cause trouble. Or –'

'That's a lot of "or"s,' interrupts Oti. 'And what of those . . . things we saw in the parlour?'

I pull a pillow to my lap and sink my face into it. 'They're another *or*,' I mutter, dejected. 'I read a bit about them in the Book of Devona . . . it's like our bible, a journal written by Devona women over the years. Those shapes and streamer-like things? I haven't seen them before. They were spirits, though. Caught between here and . . . there.'

'Does it say anything in the book about how it could have happened?' asks Cecily.

'I only wish I could remember! There's a passage about it being a door rarely opened, or suchlike, and a warning that it shouldn't be done, that the forces are too strong. Gosh, I wish I could remember more, but I read it years ago now.'

'It happened the moment Oti took your hand,' observes Cecily quietly.

'That's true,' I say, 'and it mentioned linking hands in the book too, but I've held hands with people before and nothing's happened.' I smile, before confessing: 'I've tried to do it, a few times.'

'Why would you want to do that?' asks Cecily.

'I don't know. Boredom? There isn't a whole lot to do in the middle of the countryside.'

'It would certainly add an element of peril to ring-a-ring o' roses,' says Oti.

Cecily snorts. 'Surely there are less terrifying activities than trying to open a gateway into a realm of potentially harmful spirits? What's wrong with knitting?'

'Do you know what tries my nerves?' I say, suddenly angry. 'The fact that I have this supposed gift and yet it's no help whatsoever! Even the meddling you do at your fake seances is more use!'

'What do you mean?' Oti asks.

'You know full well what I mean! That awful woman who wanted to contest her mother's will to stop the money going to charity? You certainly gave her something to think about! Your pretend spirits are more help than my real ones!'

The room slips sideways.

Oti and I lock eyes. She nods slowly. 'Of course.' A smile slips across her face. 'My goodness. Of course!'

'Of course what?' asks Cecily. 'What are you two smiling about?'

Excitement swarms through me and I root around in my carpet bag for a pencil.

Guest list, I write on a fresh page in my journal, underlining it three times.

'Right,' I say. 'Oti . . . Cecily: we are going to throw the best fake seance the world has ever seen.'

I have been lying awake for hours, buzzing with new energy.

I make my way downstairs, tasked with finding names of those we are to invite to our fake seance to save Sally. It's an address book I'm after, and that will likely be in Mr Bletchley's study. I would ask him directly, but I feel certain that he'd find this new plan even less agreeable, given that he's adamant I shouldn't draw attention to myself. It's odd how, on this issue, he and my father are of exactly the same opinion.

I wait for Mr Bletchley to leave before letting myself in. The fire is low and offers little in the way of light, but I daren't open the curtains. From what I can see, it is a pleasing room, with wood-panelled walls that glint golden in the firelight, like slabs of toffee before you smash them to smithereens with a tiny silver hammer.

The desk is a mess. There are documents *everywhere*. I scrabble through sheaves of papers as if I'm delving into a lucky dip and, eventually, I come across a very smart address book, its foolscap-sized pages bound in navy leather. I give a little whoop of triumph and flick through it to make sure it holds the information I need, and out flutters what looks like a tiny greetings card about the size of a matchbox. I hold it up to the fire to get a better look.

The front of the card is bone white with a design picked out in black ink – the outline of an eye, with a cross, gothic in style, above it. Printed within the cross are two words – 'THE' set horizontally, and 'RIGHTEOUS' vertically, intersecting at the 'E'. The Righteous. The temperature in the room drops. With trembling fingers, I open the card and read: *Hand her over.*

Breath catches in my throat and I step back, as if burned by the message. I know it means me. I *know* it. I have to get out of here. I slot the card back between the pages of the address book, take a shaky step towards the door and then pause as my eye is caught by a piece of parchment on the floor, semi-transparent, the colour of a tea stain and curled at the corners. There's something drawn on it; it's a diagram. I can't make out much in the gloom, but there are lines and some fancy script and what looks like a name at the top: *D E V O*–

Thud thud thud.

No! Someone's coming!

I fall to my knees and shuffle towards the curtains, address book tucked under one arm. I make it to safety barely a half second before the door opens. Scrabbling my nightgown tight round me, I peek through the curtain fringing, trying to quieten my breathing as blood thumps in my ears.

Dotty.

Sweat prickles under my arms. Dotty has come, no doubt, to prepare the room for the day. Setting the fire anew, dusting the grate, opening the curt– *Oh no!* What if she discovers me? I swallow. But Dotty doesn't hasten to her tasks. Instead, she performs the same dance as I've just done, casting her gaze over the desk, pushing documents out of the way, lifting papers. And then she walks across to the hearth and takes something out of her apron pocket. It's the morning post. By sleuthing in here,

I've missed it. Dotty peers at the envelopes, tilting them towards the fire to try to get a better look. She squints, and runs a finger over them, like Sally used to do before she could –

Of course. Pity rushes through me. *She can't read.*

Dotty slaps at her forehead with the letters, grunting in frustration, and it's all I can do to stop myself betraying my hiding place and running to her. Would she accept my help? Or would she clout me with the nearest pheasant carcass and –

'Dotty? Where are you, girl?' Mrs Morris snaps from somewhere out of the room. 'Where you hidin' now?' There is a loud *yak-a-yak-ak*, like the crack of a wooden spoon on a saucepan, and Dotty pulls up, sharply, as if shot. The envelopes tumble from her grasp and, in her fluster, she knocks them towards the grate.

'M–m . . . MizMorris?' Dotty is wild-eyed, scrabbling for the dropped post. 'Ah, no!' she yelps, snatching her hand back and shoving a finger in her mouth. 'Stuff it,' she mutters, skidding like a newborn deer on the polished floorboards as she rushes for the door.

I wait a beat until her footsteps fade and run to the fire, grabbing the glass of water from the desk as I pass. I fish the envelopes out with the coal tongs and douse them with water. They're charred, but the writing is still legible, the grease from Dotty's fingers having formed a protective smear. Most are for Mr Bletchley. But one is addressed to me – and it's from the gaol! A letter from Sally.

I fly up to my room, peeling open the envelope as I run, not caring if I'm heard, and sit cross-legged on the floor, smoothing the letter out with my hands, crying out in frustration as the edges pull away and disintegrate – some lines of her beautiful script are legible, but not all. Ink leaches into the white paper and I blot at it with the edge of my nightgown, desperate to save what I can, for with every lost word a piece of Sally disappears. And then I read.

Dearest Peggy,

Your note lifted my harte so! I know you are trying to help me. You will, won't you? For I am propper scared of that rope, Peg.

Look at you at Traiter Bl... is after all you s...

Be careful, though. I heard ... trusted! I Had ideas above my stay shun, the little weasel, said ... lot down a notch or two.

Plese get me out of here, Peg! The only
visiter I have i[...]

Makes me wish for
solitude. I am disowned by my family
And if I confess I
then I'll be spared t[...]
[...]ure. I believe [...] killed her? But
I would [...] been as. You must
promise me that it'll be you I see if
die, that it'll be you I see on my
burn. That yours will be the last [...]
I see. Your (best! Always!) friend
Sally Hubbard

I run a finger over her signature, and a tremor of
terror judders through me, as if her fear has jumped
into me. '*I killed her.*' The words leaps out at me. I
hold the letter to the light, in the hope I can read the
smudged lines more clearly, but I can't. That isn't
what she means, I know it. Don't I? As for this cruel
visitor – they will pay for their lies, whoever they are.

I transcribe the names and addresses that I need
from Mr Bletchley's book to my journal, then

quickly run down to his study to replace it on his desk.

Back in my room once more, I sit on my bed, going over and over Sally's words and trying – and failing – to push away the feeling that something terrible is going to happen.

22

Hours pass. Cecily and Oti have been out and I've seen nothing of Mr Bletchley. I busied myself with writing invitations, the girls having provided official emporium stationery for the task, but my head aches from worry. Worry about Sally, worry about the plan, but also worry about that horrible little card, which looks bigger and scarier to me with every fretful look I give it. I couldn't help but keep it when I returned the address book. Who are 'The Righteous'? And those chilling words: '*Hand her over.*' Is it really me that they wish Mr Bletchley to hand over? What do they want with me? And how can I possibly ask him without him knowing I've been snooping around in his private office?

It is late evening, and growls from my stomach remind me I've missed supper, so I pad downstairs from my room in stockinged feet. There is usually a plate of cold meats in the kitchen, or at least some bread and butter, laid out under cloths in the cold store. I keep an eye out for Mrs Morris, for although she doesn't really bother me I'd prefer not to see her.

I walk past the photographs with their friendly little glowing dots, ignore the creepy paintings, nod a greeting to the wall of masks, and wave to the strange, suspended creatures in their specimen-jar homes. Three steps down the staircase and I stop. Muffled voices – Bletchley's deep, rounded tones and another voice – are coming from Mr Bletchley's private quarters.

'This is monstrous!'

'Don't be ridiculous, Bletchley. I am confounded as to why you would challenge me so.'

Bletchley's voice is icy cold. 'I simply wanted more information. If everything is above board, I can see no reason for you to be concerned.'

'Oh, Bletchley, please! You've obviously lost all reason. I'm saving you from yourself, sir! You'll become a laughing stock if you pursue this. It's a sorry business, of course.' A theatrical sigh. 'I gain no pleasure from it.'

'I wish I could believe that,' says Mr Bletchley.

'I'm sorry to have to say this, Jedediah, but if you don't leave well alone I'll have no option but to exert my influence, as I said before. A word in the right ear will be enough and I'm sure you don't want that.'

'But that . . . that is blackmail!'

'I wish there were another way. But you've brought this on yourself. No, don't get up. I'll see myself out.'

I swallow, icy fear pricking at my scalp. That voice . . . That dull, droning voice . . .

I scuttle back up to the landing and crawl to the waiting area, squashing myself between the spinning wheel and the enormous curiosity cabinet. A bead of sweat trickles down my back, and I tuck my pinafore under my knees, leaning forward, pushing my head between two upright posts of the banister. In doing so, my elbow accidentally knocks against the spinning wheel and it rocks unsteadily. I grab it to steady it; my fingers curl round the smooth wooden spokes and –

Argh! . . . My back! . . . *Swish!* . . . *SLAP!* A whip whistles through the air, cracking against my back again and again and again. I curl up like a hedgehog. *What's happening?* The pain steals my breath and I'm there, in the workhouse, listening to the wheel *click, click, click,* the whip *swish, swish, swish.* Hunger twists my gut, and a desolate, aching sadness in my heart sends me sinking down and down and down. *Let go,* I tell myself. *You have to LET GO!* And I send all my mind to my hand, to my fingers, where knotted wood melds to skin, and I imagine them pulling away one by one from the wood. *Let go, let go . . . NOW! Uuuurgh!* I fall backwards, drenched in sweat, panting and terrified. *What. Just. Happened?* I've never experienced anything like that before, ever. The spirits here are so much stronger! Or is it . . . me?

But there is no time to work it out. Mr Bletchley's door clicks open. A small bell rings. A gas lamp casts a yolky glow directly in my eyeline and I squint to rid myself of the glare, dark spots dancing in my vision. I hold my breath. 'The girl will bring your coat. You won't get away with this,' says Bletchley flatly.

He doesn't respond, this other man, whose profile is sharp and bird-like, his tall, thin frame dressed entirely in black: a frock coat, a wide-brimmed hat.

A flash of white at his throat. The world tunnels in on me.

Reverend Silas Tate. The vicar. But . . . why?

The moment Mr Bletchley returns to his rooms, a shape peels from the wall. Dotty slips from the shadows to Mr Tate's side, passing him his coat and scuttling along next to him as he walks to the front door. I should warn her about him, but what would I say? The door opens, it closes, and I unfold, a faint keening noise giving me pause, but I hurry away, face burning with the shame of overhearing Mr Bletchley, a grown man, softly crying behind his door.

23

The following morning I wake before dawn, head throbbing. Through the attic window a pitch-black sky slides into the peach-washed grey of morning, a brief flush of optimism before the air fills with the threat of rain and all I can see is ashen drabness once more.

I don't know what to do. I barely know my own name, leaden as I am from lack of sleep. What happened when I touched the spinning wheel? What was Mr Tate doing here? And why did it upset Mr Bletchley so?

I don't have time for this.

Tomorrow night, I am to channel Sally's supposed victim, Lady Stanton, to have her tell the assembled group that she most definitely was *not* murdered, and that Sally is an innocent victim in all this. My initial optimism is fading, and rapidly. Even if I can convince everyone in attendance of Sally's innocence, the words of a psychic – real, fake or otherwise – would not be taken seriously in a court of law, and the absolute best I can hope for is that we can plant enough doubt in people's minds to ensure that the matter is investigated further. It's a thin plan, to say the least, but it's all we have.

I splash my face with water from the washbasin, the biting cold slapping my face awake. A noise outside, a clatter of . . . what? Rain? Hail? I pull over the chair to stand on and press my face to the window, but although the sky foretells rain it's yet to release its burden.

Crack.

The glass splinters, a jagged rift appearing across the pane. I open the window and stick my head out just as a stone hits me on the side of the head. 'Oi!' I shout, looking down. 'Who's that? Stop it!'

The square is near deserted, save for a man shovelling horse dung on to a barrow and a couple of delivery carts. Someone is waving from the pavement opposite the house, in front of the gated gardens. Waving and theatrically gesturing towards the back of the house. From up here it looks like they're on strings, like a puppet. But it's no puppet.

It's Ambrose.

I fly downstairs. I meet him at the tradesman's entrance, between the side of the scullery and the coach house, the aroma of baking bread competing with the tang of warm horse dung, and I throw my arms round his neck.

'*Oof!* Steady, old thing!' he says.

I can't let him go – I have to tell him everything, all of it, *right now*. 'I can't believe you're here,' I rattle on. 'There's so much to tell you! I have a plan – we're doing a fake seance and – oh, have you heard of "The Righteous"? Because I think they may be after me ... No? ... Anyway, me and Cecily and Oti are going to fake a visit from Lady Stanton's spirit and tell everyone that Sally is innocent and then they'll have to let her go, *surely* they'll let her go. They will, won't they? They'll believe it all and then they'll let her go.' I stop, my words catching up with me.

I slump against Ambrose's brocade jacket, the heavy silk cool against my tired face. 'They won't believe it, will they?' I mumble. 'It's not going to work.' A sob spools up from my chest. 'You got the letter to her. Thank you. She replied but Dotty dropped it in the fire – accidentally, I *think* – and I can only read half of it, but thank you,' I say between sobs.

He peels me off him and holds me by the shoulders. 'Look, Peggy –' He pauses and I move my gaze up from his fancy clothes – apple-green jacket, lemon-posset waistcoat, cherry cravat – to his face. There's a bruise on his temple, red and tender-looking against his parchment-coloured skin.

'Oh, Ambrose . . . who's done that to you?'

'It's nothing.' A tear slides down his cheek and my heart twists like a dishrag.

'Did Bletchley strike you?' I ask.

'Goodness me, no, he wouldn't do that.' He grips my hands in his. 'It's happened, Peg.'

His words are a slap. 'What? What's happened?' I say nervously.

'Sally's trial. It happened yesterday.' He looks at me, wipes at his face with the back of his hand. 'They say she's guilty, Peg. They say Sally's a murderer. It was a closed court. She had no one to speak up for her. She confessed, Peggy. Said she did it. It's over. Sally's going to swing.'

*

The taste of vomit hits my throat and I heave again, nothing but stinging bile left in my gullet.

'She can't have confessed, she can't have!' Gravel digs into my knees as I sit back on my haunches.

Ambrose passes me a handkerchief to wipe my mouth, waving it away as I move to hand it back to him.

'Why? Why is he letting it happen?'

'Bletchley, you mean?' Ambrose shrugs, sitting gingerly on a steel garden roller propped against the scullery wall. 'He's not as influential as he likes to make out. Matters of criminal law are nothing to do with him. He came to see me late last night. He's a broken man, Peggy. He says he's going to have to stop the seance.'

'What? No! I mean, how does he even know about it? You wait until I see him! What a ridiculous –' I stop. Realization dawns on me. 'Tate was here. Bletchley was upset. That must have been before he came to see you.'

'Mr Tate paid me a visit too. Asking questions.'

'What about?'

'You, Peggy.'

This throws me. 'What sort of questions about me?'

'About what I knew about your skills . . . Don't worry,' he says, holding his hands up as I open my mouth to protest. 'I told him nothing. He also wanted to know why I'd been passing a letter to a known murderer.'

'What? How did he know about that?'

'I have no idea. He wasn't very happy about any of it.' Ambrose lifts a hand to his bruise.

'*He* hit you. Mr Tate.'

He nods. 'I told him that the rumours about you were just that: made-up nonsense, spread about for larks. You know he was behind those posters in Alderley?'

'What do you mean? I thought those posters were everywhere.' I look around, stupidly, as if expecting to see one in the yard.

'No,' confirms Ambrose. 'They're nowhere else. Only in our village. It seems likely that the graffiti about you was also his handiwork.'

'But after what happened to the whisperling up north last year . . . the one who was drowned,' I say.

'There was no attack up north. There haven't been any in a long, long time.'

'But the posters,' I insist, 'they're to remind folk to *not* treat whisperlings badly. I don't understand.'

Ambrose shrugs. 'Are they, though? Because what do they actually say? Report anyone who is being mean to a whisperling? That could be quite a clever way of –'

'Finding out who the whisperlings are!' I gasp.

'Exactly. If they asked people to report anyone they thought had the gift, well, it wouldn't work, not now. "Don't be a snitch, you might kill a witch" – wasn't that what they used to say in the old days?'

I take in everything he says. 'So Silas Tate is blackmailing Mr Bletchley, forcing him into silence about Sally.'

Ambrose nods. 'And if Jed tries to help Sally, then someone else will get hurt. You, presumably. He was truly beside himself, said he was "damned either way" – I'm sorry about his coarse language, Peggy. Anyway, I told him to do whatever you said.'

Warmth spreads through my heart and melts more tears from my eyes. 'You did?'

'I did. Look, I know you won't agree, but Mr Bletchley isn't a bad man. I know you think he's a traitor because he defied your pa and tried to make money out of the whisperling gift and all that . . . You can roll your eyes all you want, Peggy, but he *isn't* bad. I'm not necessarily saying he's a *good* man. I mean, he isn't like your father, for example. But he isn't evil. Not like . . .'

'Tate.'

His name hangs between us, leaching out dark threads of menace and fear.

Ambrose has gone, but with a promise to return tomorrow. It's early, but I can't wait any longer.

Rat-a-tat-tat.

'Mr Bletchley? Can I come in?'

'Go away.'

I open the door. 'Mr Bletchley?'

It's very dark and I take a moment to become accustomed to the gloom. I walk towards the drawn curtains with my arms outstretched and drag open a heavy velvet panel. The room immediately brightens, revealing Mr Bletchley at his desk, still in his pyjamas. He removes his blue-and-white-striped nightcap and blinks into the daylight.

'I'm sorry you have to see me like this, Peggy.'

'And I'm sorry that my best friend is likely to die soon, Mr Bletchley,' I reply.

I regret it, instantly, as he throws his head down on to his desk and sobs, great viscous heaves of molten sorrow. '*Harrumphhht!* Oh, do excuse me,' he says, as he blows his nose into his nightcap. Dotty will be on laundry duty. The thought cheers me, slightly.

'There, there, Mr Bletchley,' I say soothingly.

I look around as he neatens himself. It's an agreeable room – one wall is given over entirely to books; there is even a little ladder for reaching the higher shelves. There are papers strewn everywhere, but I can't see the interesting-looking parchment I saw before. I notice, though, a wooden box, filled to the brim with photographs.

Mr Bletchley leans heavily on his elbows, covering his face with his hands, pushing them under his glasses until the frames rest on his fingers. His crying has subsided but his voice still catches on every word. 'I-I'm s-so s-sorry, P-Peggy.'

'Mr Bletchley, please try and pull yourself together!' I urge. 'We need clear heads if we're to be of any use to anyone. We'll cry later if we have to.'

He looks at me like a lot of people do. 'You're a funny little thing, aren't you?'

I shrug. 'So I've heard.'

'This wasn't how things were supposed to be; you must believe me, Peggy.'

I take a seat opposite him. 'What do you mean?'

He leans back in his chair and sighs. 'I am full of big ideas, Peggy. The Psychic Emporium was supposed to be the crowning glory of my career. I wanted to bring the skills of all the whisperlings out into the light, to help people connect with their loved ones and bring peace to their lives.' He nods towards the box of photographs. 'And I wanted to take images of the spirits too, to have proof of the afterlife.' He raises an eyebrow. 'It's a load of old rubbish, of course, but I still do it now, just in case . . . silly old fool that I am. Can't get anything right, can I?'

I say nothing, wondering again about the little lights I see in the photographs on the landing.

He continues. 'I wanted the skill of the whisperlings to be accepted by the scientists, so that it could be harnessed and used for the greater good, to unravel mysteries, to solve crimes.' He sighs, and slumps in his chair like a deflated bag of flour. 'Unfortunately, of those I tracked down, not one true whisperling would work for me, not that any were even halfway gifted, truth be told. Not one was like you, that's for certain. You know, Peggy, it was clear from the moment you came here that your gift is growing ever stronger – first the incident at Clifton Bridge, then after your first seance, the one with the Gradys. You'll be seeing ghosts all over the place before you know it.'

I don't respond.

He continues. 'However honourable my intentions, I regret to say the emporium is little more than a sham. Whisperlings are not given to theatrics, it would seem.'

I snort. 'Well, I could've told you that.'

'Your father did. Many, many . . . many times.'

'Is that why he banished you?' I ask.

He bristles. 'He didn't *banish* me. It was a disagreement, after which it was suggested that I keep my distance. Your father was more traditional in his outlook – you more than anyone know about that, what with all the hoo-ha over the Book of Devona – whereas I wanted to move with the times, be more . . . progressive.'

'You should have listened to Pa,' I say quietly, unsettled by all this Devona talk with someone I don't consider to be truly family.

'I most certainly should have done,' he replies. 'He was so in tune with it all, while to me it felt so abstract, like make-believe. Did you know that our mother, Vada, died not long after your father was born?'

I nod, remembering the painting of Granny Vada on the parlour wall.

'John was sent to stay with our mother's family, who were all Devona, of course, so Father could work. I stayed with Father, being that much older and more useful around the place than a baby. Little wonder, therefore, that out of the two of us John was chosen to keep the Devona name.'

'"Chosen to keep the name"?' I say, puzzled. 'What do you mean?'

'You didn't know? Our father's surname was Bletchley. But the tradition is (and it's written somewhere) that the Devona name must be carried on whenever possible and is therefore passed down to a child or children. In most cases, it will go to a daughter, should there be one.'

'But why,' I ask, 'seeing as the Devona legacy runs through the female line, didn't Grandad Bletchley take Granny Vada's name – surely that would have been simpler?'

Mr Bletchley looks at me as if I have sprouted an extra head. 'That's ridiculous! What, a man take his wife's last name? You really *are* a funny sausage,' and he dismisses my suggestion with a flick of his snotty handkerchief. 'In order for the Devona name to continue, in cases such as ours, when there was no female to inherit it, the name is passed on, not to the eldest child, but to the most . . . worthy.'

'Pa,' I whisper.

Mr Bletchley nods. 'I was young, and angry and foolish. I felt like your father had taken everything from me: our mother, although of course that wasn't his fault; my Devona birthright, even though I didn't really want it; and then, finally –' He stops himself.

'Finally what?'

'I've said too much,' says Mr Bletchley, looking ruffled. 'Needless to say, I fear that in my eagerness to seek revenge on my little brother I've made everything so much worse.'

'How so?'

'My overseas emporiums were targeted by some sort of anti-whisperling group. As it was, I had no whisperlings actually working for me, but they didn't know that and the threats were worrying –

zealots will string up anyone once they've tasted blood. So I shut the lot down apart from the Bristol emporium, assuming that good old England would be far too civilized for such nonsense.' He shakes his head ruefully. 'But how wrong I was.'

'Is it "The Righteous" who are behind all this?' I ask.

'How *on earth* do you know about them?' He is aghast, so I tell him about the note I found in his address book. 'I see,' he says sternly. 'Well, we'll discuss your snooping another time, Peggy, but, yes, it would appear that, far from being an issue I only had to face overseas, The Righteous – whoever they are – are here in England. And I've led them straight to you. I don't know what to do; I really don't.'

'I'm not cancelling the seance!' I say fiercely.

'No, I didn't expect you to, not for one moment.' He smiles to himself. 'You're a Devona. We're a stubborn lot. And it's a good idea.' He sighs. 'It's certainly got Mr Tate rattled. He got wind of it somehow and made some pretty terrible threats about what he would do if I didn't cancel.'

'Mr Tate,' I whisper.

Bletchley nods. 'Yes, Mr Tate, the vicar.' A vein pulses in his temple. 'Mr Tate, the star witness.'

His words are a slap. *Star witness . . . Of course!*

Mr Bletchley hesitates, pulling at the corners of his moustache. 'And you're absolutely sure about Sally, are you –'

'She didn't do it.'

'But the confession . . .?'

'She didn't do it. I know you're trying to prepare me in case . . . the worst happens. But she didn't do it. The confession is false or they must have forced her to sign it.' *Oh, Sally! My dear, sweet friend, what did they do to you to get you to confess?*

His eyes shine with tears but to my relief he keeps them in check. 'I'm so sorry, Peggy. I've failed you. You're a child. I'm a grown man. It was down to me to resolve the situation.'

I raise an eyebrow. 'And now?'

'And now I know better.' He removes his glasses, wipes his face with his sleeve and sits up, straight and determined. 'What do you want me to do?'

'Right, Mr Bletchley,' I say with renewed purpose. 'I need you to deliver some invitations. We have a fake seance to perform.'

The last of the invitations – a smart navy card, embossed in gold with the same eye and crown logo as the emporium's business cards – had been delivered. The one for Governor Jones was posted through the door of his country retreat, less than three miles but a world away from the stench of Bristol Gaol.

The plan remains the same – to convince these influential people of Sally's innocence, but now she's been convicted the stakes are even higher. Somehow, we must persuade them there's been a terrible miscarriage of justice.

All invitations were accepted, although Governor Jones has sent Mr Craven, the deputy prison governor, in his place. Mr Percival Craven is an unexpectedly jolly man with a thunderclap laugh and candyfloss hair. 'Good to finally meet you, Bletchley! This is Jemima, my wife . . . she's quite a fan of yours. Fair to say, since your invitation arrived, she has never been more pleased to have married me!' he says, greeting Mr Bletchley with a vigorous handshake, his wife nodding and smiling nervously at his side. She's a sweet-looking woman about the same age as my mother. She wears a small black bonnet and her face is framed by tight, neat ringlets that remind me of strings of skinny sausages. 'Rather looking forward to it myself, I must say,' the deputy governor continues. 'A welcome distraction, as it were.' He wears a monocle, which he pops in and out when he talks, although he hasn't spoken to me at all. Young girls are the ghosts of society, it seems.

Everyone is here. Cecily and Oti, of course, and Mr Bletchley and Ambrose, and we have been joined for the evening by our four esteemed guests: Mr Linworth, the stipendiary magistrate, and Mr Balfour Emery from the *Bristol Evening Post*, as well as Mr and Mrs Craven. It was Mr Bletchley's idea to invite the journalist, thinking it wouldn't do any harm to have someone present with an eye for a story and a nose for irregularity.

'There's no way I'd pass this up!' Emery said when Mr Bletchley thanked him for coming. 'Your evenings are the hot ticket. Talk of the town, they are! Never thought a hack like me'd get an invite. Sharpened my pencil specially, I have.'

'I hope you get a story worthy of the front page,' replied Bletchley, raising an eyebrow in my direction. He is risking so much – a poor story from this reporter would ruin him. I take a deep breath. We *have* to get this right.

Mr Bletchley guides us from the waiting area and the chatter increases as the cogs of excitement tighten up a notch.

The guests pause at the curiosity cabinet, thrilled: 'Is that . . . brain?'

'Urgh, you wouldn't want to find that poor creature in your pickle jar, would you?'

'Oh my, look at those tiny skulls! One could wear them as earrings!'

As we enter the parlour, there is a palpable intake of breath. Waist-high church candles edge the room, casting a buttery glow over the velvet curtains and throwing shadows against the panelled walls.

'Shall we?' says Oti, gesturing towards the table, which is covered in heavy black cloth and set with a jug of water, drinking glasses and a vase of headily scented flowers – roses, violets, lavender. The smell is achingly familiar and, for a moment, I am back home, back in the dressing room with Mama, washing down a body with lavender-scented water. Sally's face flashes in front of me – is it her body I see? No. *No!* I push away the image as we take our seats.

Oti, Cecily and I are seated between Mr Bletchley, Ambrose, Mr Craven and his wife (who is now nervous beyond patience), Mr Linworth and Mr Emery. I smooth my skirts, pray for my heart to stop beating so loudly and wait for the nervous laughter of the group to settle. We are dressed in black – Cecily, Oti and myself – although under the cape Cecily has lent me I'm wearing my mother's dark-blue dress. Oti has rolled and pinned my hair. Should anything happen, I need to be taken seriously – if I owned a man's suit, I'd have worn that.

Suddenly warm, I remove the cape, folding and placing it under my chair, neatening the collar on Mama's dress as I sit back down. I tap my head, pushing back a wayward pin. My hair is lumpen and uncomfortable and I can't wait to release it. I catch Mr Bletchley looking at my dress, his expression odd. If I didn't know better, I'd say he's seen a ghost.

Mr Linworth the magistrate and Mr Craven the deputy governor are my targets. I need to unsettle them enough to make them at least reopen Sally's case, if not throw it out completely. Mr Linworth is hard to read, and has said little so far this evening. He's the only one who doesn't seem excited to be here. He removes his spectacles and rubs them on his ochre woollen waistcoat. His attire is as conservative as his manner, unlike Bletchley, whose frock coat and silk cravat, albeit dishevelled, give him the appearance of someone who is always ready for the opera.

I nod at Cecily.

'Shall we begin? We must hold hands, all of us,' she says, in that low, inviting voice of hers. Mr Emery the reporter and Mr Craven are seated one on either side of her, and already they are transfixed. Her dress this evening is a simple column of black with a small bustle at the back, and long, full-length, narrow sleeves ending in a point on the back of each hand. Her shoulders are entirely bare and a slick of rose oil on her collarbones shimmers in the lamplight.

'Are there any spirits near who wish to communicate?' she calls. 'We are open and ready.' Then she stills for a moment, waits until all eyes are upon her, and tips back her head as if in rapture, exposing her milky-white throat.

A rhythm begins, a *ching-ching* of tiny bells – altar bells that Oti taps with her foot under the table. A waft of incense rises from the burner on the floor and I try not to breathe in too heavily, for I suspect from the sweet tang in the air that there may be some of Cecily's 'special powder' mixed in with the resin.

Cecily sways, very gently, very slowly, a mesmerizing motion that takes the room with her. '*Uuuuh*,' she moans softly. '*Uuuuh*.'

Oti now. '*Ohhhm-an-ne-ya, ohm-an-ne-ya,*' she intones, almost to herself at first, a misty hum gradually becoming louder until there is no space in my head for anything else.

'O spirits, dear departed souls, we are open for you. Come to us, be among us, let me channel you.' Cecily's voice is husky, barely more than a whisper.

In the corner of the parlour I see a boy.

As clear as day he is to me, dressed in a ragged smock, his feet bare, skinny as a whippet, holding a rock bigger than his head. The stench of rotten meat makes me gag – it must be from that pile of bones at his feet. He crouches, lifts the rock above his head and thuds it to the floor. 'Crunch,' I say.

'I beg your pardon?' says Mr Linworth.

'Crunch,' I repeat. 'Crunch, crunch, crunch. Over and over and over and over.'

'Are you quite all right, Peggy?' I look at Mr Bletchley, who asked me the question, but I can barely focus. It's as if he's behind a screen. 'Peggy?' he repeats.

'Bone crushing. He does it all day. Till he drops.'

'Who?'

'Him, there.' I nod towards the boy – can't they see him? Are they blind? 'Crunch, crunch, crunch. It was him, his ma an' his baby brother, but they got the pox so now it's only h-him.' My voice catches. 'If he stops working, they'll chuck him out. He ain't got time to cry.'

'Beckford Square was built on the site of a workhouse,' Mr Bletchley explains from far away. 'I suspect Miss Devona is . . . sensing something from that time.'

'Very clever,' says Mr Emery. 'Verifiable detail, very clever indeed.'

'No fun if we can't see anything, though!' says Mr Craven. 'Show me the ectoplasm!'

'Don't be disrespectful, Percival,' hisses his wife.

'My apologies, Jemima dear.'

'Peggy?' Cecily says. 'Come back to us. You need to control this. Fill your mind, remember?'

She's right, I know she's right, but the *crunch, crunch, crunch* of rock against bone is getting louder and louder and – 'Ouch!' I rub at my cheek. 'You pinched me!'

'Sorry,' says Ambrose. 'It seemed like the right thing to do.' He doesn't look particularly sorry, but I don't care. The boy in the corner has gone.

Mr Bletchley coughs and dabs at his forehead with his handkerchief. 'The spirits are unpredictable tonight.' We exchange a look. He was right – my gift is getting stronger.

The room is thick with heady, amber-tinged smoke.

'There is energy around us . . . Can you feel it?' intones Cecily, and everyone nods, even dry Mr Linworth.

Oti's chanting becomes louder and the *ching-ching* of the altar bells increases in tempo until there is only a constant rolling chime.

'O spirits, are you with us?' Cecily begs. The table lurches and Mrs Craven yelps, reeling back in her seat. There are shouts and shrieks as it tips again. Even I scream despite knowing that Oti and Ambrose are doing this, pushing up the lightweight tabletop with spiky hooks attached to their belts.

The atmosphere is charged.

It's time.

'Excuse me, I must get my handkerchief,' I whisper to Mrs Craven, releasing my hand from hers. I quickly remove two pins from my hair to allow it to fall round my shoulders, then turn to Ambrose, who dabs my face with white greasepaint from the pot he has concealed up his sleeve, and finally I throw a veil of black netting over my head. All the while, Cecily moans, Oti chants and no one looks at me. Transformation complete, I slide my hand back into Mrs Craven's.

Cecily's head snaps up. 'There is someone here,' she declares.

'My name is Lady Victoria Stanton.' My voice shakes – it is high-pitched and reedy, and I sound nothing like myself.

Mrs Craven dares a glance at me. 'It's – it's . . . a spectre! A spectre, beside me, here in this room! Percy, Percy, it's a spectre!'

I could hug her.

'What do you want from us, Lady Stanton?' says Cecily.

'I have an important message,' I say.

'As you wish,' says Cecily. 'Please, talk to us.'

'They say I was murdered. But this is a lie.'

The room gasps. I dare a glance at Mr Linworth, the magistrate, sitting there between Mr Bletchley and Mrs Craven, but he is unreadable. 'There is no mystery, no drama. I simply . . . died.'

'But, Lady Stanton,' says Mr Craven, 'there was a trial . . .'

'A closed trial, to my knowledge,' I say.

'Eh? It was a closed trial? Why ever was that?' Mr Emery, the journalist, asks. 'That sounds a little unusual.'

The magistrate clears his throat. 'It was clear that the girl was guilty. We had certain . . . evidence.'

'I'm afraid you're mistaken, Your Honour,' I say, struggling to keep hold of myself. 'The evidence you say you have must be wrong, as there could be no evidence since there was no murder. Your witness is lying.'

'How do you know about the witness?' snaps the magistrate.

'I am everywhere. I see *everything*,' I improvise. 'Sally is just a child, Mr Linworth.'

'A child who signed a confession and that's the end of the matter.'

'No! She wouldn't have!' I feel Ambrose squeeze my hand, but I can't calm myself down. 'She wouldn't have signed a confession unless she was forced!' I insist, struggling to keep up my ghostly persona.

'I've heard enough. This is a ridiculous charade!' says Mr Linworth, shaking his hands free and rising to his feet.

'The chain!' says Mr Bletchley. 'Don't break the chain!'

Mr Linworth tuts at Mr Bletchley's plea. 'Can you not see you are being manipulated, you fools? I confess I found her earlier performance quite convincing, but this girl is no more Lady Stanton than I am the Queen of Sheba!'

I can't breathe. 'Sally was my lady's maid. I would urge you to re-examine the case. I was –' my voice cracks – 'very fond of her.'

'I'm sure you were, *Lady* Stanton,' Mr Linworth says sarcastically. 'I can't imagine you'd have left your fortune to her if you weren't.'

The room tilts sharply away. I may faint.

'She . . . what?' says Mr Bletchley, glaring at Mr Linworth. 'Sally was mentioned in Lady Stanton's will?'

Mr Linworth shuffles uncomfortably. 'I'm not at liberty to discuss —'

'Oh, Mr Linworth,' Mr Bletchley exclaims, cutting him off. 'I believe we're past any pretence of that sort. I suspect you've already told us more than your job's worth. If you prefer, I could always contact your superiors for clarification?'

Mr Linworth slumps back down in his chair. 'No, there's no need for that. Besides which, this so-called information is irrelevant. Sally Hubbard is guilty. We have her confession, signed with an X. Case closed.'

The room stills as his words catch up with me. 'Wait a moment . . . what did you say?' I look round at Mrs Craven and withdraw my hand from her grip. 'I'm sorry, Mrs Craven, I'm not really a spirit, and anyone who says they are is having you on.'

'I know that, dear – I'm not daft.' She winks at me and I feel a rush of affection for her. 'And as for you, Mr Linworth,' Mrs Craven continues, 'there's nothing wrong with asking questions. Perhaps if you stopped presuming you knew everything already, you'd learn something important.'

'Oh, very well,' says Mr Linworth with a huff. 'Miss Hubbard had the confession read to her and she signed her agreement to it with an –'

'With an X.' I roll my eyes in exasperation as I finish his sentence. 'Yes, so you said.'

He laughs harshly. 'So what exactly are you not understanding, little girl? It isn't complica–'

'Sally can read and write.'

If I slapped him, he'd not look as shocked as he does now. 'Well, I don't know about that,' he finally manages to say.

'No? But I do. I know. My mother taught her.' I stand and reach into my skirts to pull out Sally's letter. 'Look! This is from her! This is her writing! And you can make out the prison stamp on the front, which *proves* it's from her! She wouldn't need anything to be read to her – and there's no way she'd sign anything with a simple X. No way at all.'

I pause, brain ticking. 'Who was it that supposedly read her confession to her?'

Mr Linworth swallows. 'Someone of unquestionable morals. A priest.'

A priest. Of course. My head swims and I sit down, hard.

Oti leans forward, in front of Mr Bletchley, and fixes Mr Linworth with a stare. 'Who exactly would benefit if Sally were unable to claim her inheritance?'

'Same as in most cases,' the magistrate replies. 'The Church.'

The room seems to spin and then stills. The five of us – myself, Oti, Ambrose, Mr Bletchley and Cecily – lock eyes. It's as if we have stepped out of the scene and are viewing it like we'd view a painting. We are all thinking the same thing. Mr Tate.

The parlour door flies open. A hawkish silhouette fills the frame. 'Is it him?' I whisper, heart thudding in my chest.

As the shape steps forward the shadow peels away, revealing a human form much smaller, much younger than Tate, but cut from the same cloth.

Dotty.

'Dotty?' There is a relieved chuckle in Mr Bletchley's voice. 'What do you want? You know not to interrupt when –'

'When you're doin' the Devil's work?' Dotty tilts her head, face pinched and pleased, like a wicked child holding a magnifying glass over an insect on a sunny day.

Mr Bletchley raises his eyebrows. 'I think that's quite enough, Dotty. I suggest you return to your room and we'll discuss this tomorrow.' His tone is level but the slight shake in his voice betrays his confusion. What on earth is she playing at?

She fixes me with the coldest glare before casting a withering look around the assembled company. 'You're being taken for fools. This is Peggy

Devona – she's a dirty, unholy creeper and in cahoots with that murderous schemer Sally Hubbard!'

'Yes, yes, yes, we're aware that Miss . . . Devona is not actually the spirit of Lady Stanton resurrected. It's gone a little past all that,' says Mr Emery irritably, flicking through his notes. 'Now, do as Mr Bletchley says and hop it, there's a good girl.'

Dotty doesn't move. Her eyes glitter with spite. 'You're all idiots,' she sneers. 'Sally Hubbard is guilty as sin. Mr Tate told me he saw it with his own eyes. They're gonna hang her and there's nothin' you can do about it!'

'Dotty, that is ENOUGH!' thunders Mr Bletchley. 'Leave this room immediately! Pack your things – you must leave at first light. I'll not have such hatred in my home. I've been unsure about you from the beginning, but now I see that your time working for the good vicar must have infected your brain somehow.'

Wait. Dotty worked for Mr Tate? At the vicarage? I look down at my hands, still gripping Sally's letter. I raise my eyes to Dotty, then wave the charred paper at her. 'She told me to be careful,' I say. 'Told me to watch out for someone.' I glare at Dotty. 'It's *you*, isn't it? Sally was trying to warn me about you!'

Dotty sneers and, although I don't believe in it, not really, I think I see the shadow of hell in her eyes. 'Say what you like, creeper, but the vicar says you'll be chucked into Bedlam, and no one will hear your lunatic ranting from there.'

Ah, so that's it. Now I understand the threat Silas Tate levelled at Mr Bletchley. Cancel the seance or Peggy gets thrown in the madhouse.

'What will you get out of it, Dotty?' I ask. 'How much money are you getting for being Tate's little snitch? Because that's what this is about, isn't it? Tate is framing Sally to get his hands on Lady Stanton's money!'

Dotty shrugs. 'I dunno what you're on about. Though standing by and allowin' an ill-educated wretch of a girl to inherit a fortune she doesn't deserve would surely be a sin in itself.' All eyes turn to her. The voice may be hers, but the words are absolutely those of the Reverend Mr Tate. Dotty's cheeks redden, knowing she's said too much.

The room falls silent as the truth sinks in. The despair on my shoulders tentatively lifts. *Hold on, Sally, hold on.*

'Well, I'll be . . .' Mr Craven says quietly. 'Would he really let an innocent girl hang for this?'

Mr Linworth speaks: 'I believe this evening has raised enough doubt to at least grant a stay of execution.'

'A stay of execution?' shouts Mr Bletchley, exasperated. 'Weren't you listening, you cloth-eared fool? Tate has made the whole thing up to get his hands on the Stanton fortune!'

Mr Linworth folds into himself. 'But he's a vicar! And how do we know this Dotty isn't working for the Hubbard girl, to throw us off the scent?'

Mr Bletchley slaps his forehead. 'Mr Craven, there has been a miscarriage of justice – we must speak to Governor Jones and stop the execution. Heavens, man, are you quite well?'

Mr Craven is as white as chalk. 'Oh dear. Oh dear me. I'm terribly sorry,' he says, wringing his hands, 'but we may be too late.'

'What do you mean?' asks Cecily, pale hand to her throat.

'There's no time,' says Mr Craven, looking at his pocket watch. 'The punishment is set for tonight. In an hour, when the bell tolls ten, she starts her last walk.'

My head lolls to my chest. *No. We're too late!*

Mr Emery gasps. 'I beg your pardon? The execution is tonight, while we are here, doing . . . this?'

'Did you know about this, Linworth?' Mr Bletchley is puce with rage.

The magistrate shakes his head. 'No, no, I did not. This is entirely unethical, Mr Craven!' he says. 'Who is overseeing it is done properly?'

'The governor is there, which is why I'm here in his place. It seemed a little strange – his desire to preside over the execution personally, I must admit, but I assumed it was to spare me the ordeal. We are not in agreement about the treatment of prisoners, particularly juveniles.' He shakes his head. 'And there must be a . . . priest there as well, of course, to give the prisoner her last rites if she so desires . . .' He brings his hands to his face. Because it is suddenly as clear to him as to all of us which particular priest will be in attendance.

'And where is that confounded girl Dotty?' barks Mr Emery. 'She must be apprehended!'

We scatter from the room and search wildly, but Dotty is nowhere to be seen.

'Mrs Morris!' I shout, and she appears immediately.

'Leave her to me,' she says, tapping her nose and disappearing through the wall, leaving nothing but a puff of flour and the faint rattle of keys.

Mr Bletchley stares at me, utterly mystified, but there is no time to explain. 'Dotty will be dealt with,' I say, my voice sounding miles away.

Mr Bletchley nods. 'To the carriages!'

27

The motion of the carriage thundering over cobbles churns my already roiling stomach and I swallow hard to push down the bile and fear.

I seek strength in thinking of my home, my family. And if tonight ends in the worst way, then I shall look after Sally, her body, because to me *she* is family. A sob catches in my chest.

No. I'll cry later.

'He knew,' I say to Mr Bletchley. 'Tate knew we would all be together tonight. Dotty must have heard us planning the fake seance, told him about it, and then somehow he got the execution arranged for this evening. She's been working for him all along! If ever I get my hands on her . . .'

Mr Bletchley shakes his head. 'She can't have gone far. Mrs Craven will have called for the constabulary by now. They'll soon find her. And it seems you may have some help with that from . . . Mrs Morris?'

I shrug.

'You know, she died over two years ago, our Mrs M. She suffered a heart attack, when bringing me a cup of tea. I had suspected she was still about, what with that confounded servant's bell ringing for no reason at all. It certainly put the wind up Dotty, the silly girl.'

Oh, Dotty, why did you do it? Mr Tate utterly brainwashed her, that is certain, but then why the performance this evening? Did a tiny bit of her want to reveal her association with him to us, knowing it might sabotage the vicar's plan, knowing we could still save Sally?

'I'll smack 'er in the chops when I get my 'ands on her, the little wretch,' says Cecily, coarser than I've ever heard her. 'Oh mercy, there it is.'

The gaol looms dark and solid, jutting up like a jagged tooth from the jaws of Spike Island. It looks like a fortress from another time.

'Put the shutters up,' says Bletchley. 'We're going past the docks. Cover your mouths.'

The stench hits the back of my throat and I gag, pulling out a handkerchief from my sleeve and squashing it against my face. It is one from home, doused with Mama's perfume before I left. The sweet scent of violets mingles with the thick, chewable smell seeping into the carriage. I shudder. The sickly smell of death is never far away.

A wooden bridge takes us over the thin strip of water that separates Spike Island from the rest of Bristol and we are here, waiting outside the gatehouse to be let in to the gaol. A crowd is gathering, mostly bawdy and drunken men, but there are women and, sickeningly, some children too. Word has got round that there's an execution tonight and they've been drawn here by some morbid fascination. Do they not care that it is a young girl at the gallows?

Wait . . . is that Mama? I crane my neck to look – yes, it is Mama! Mama and Mr Sweeting and – oh gracious goodness – Sally's parents, her pa holding himself upright and smart, one arm protectively round his wife. And, as I look, I can hardly believe my eyes, for I see what seems like half the village has come, along with a larger group of protesters, chanting and singing hymns and shaking fists and holding placards: 'Stop this barbaric practice!' 'Execution is evil!' 'Stop killing children!' Oh, what I wouldn't give to jump out of this carriage and run into Mama's arms!

There's a shout and the double gates swing open. I stick my head out of the carriage window, not caring about the stink; it's better than being inside my head, where the shadows are already rolling in, losing as I am this constant fight against spirits that nip at my mind like angry, needle-toothed creatures.

'Look at me,' says Ambrose, who sits opposite. He grabs my hand. 'Look at me, not out there.'

I trust him and so, for once, I do as I'm bid. I concentrate on his face, his lovely, kind face, and I manage to push away the shadows, but as we make our way through the open courtyard the carriage swings round and it is there, in my eyeline: a flat roof behind the mock portcullis by the entrance, a trap door yawning open into the space underneath. A wooden frame, a crossbeam on two uprights, and a noose that sways in the breeze, entirely benign until it tightens round the neck of a fourteen-year-old girl.

*

With Mr Craven leading the way, we run through the prison, boots clattering on slick stone floors, until we arrive at a small, dark room close to Governor Jones's office. There is a chill in this mournful space, little more than ten feet square, no source of light bar a paraffin lamp and, set in the door, a grubby glazed window laced with metal bars. There is a compact table and four chairs and a jug half full of water floating with green scum. The lime-washed walls are slick with moisture. My chest tightens. People have died in here, but at the moment all the spirits seem to be settled, thank goodness. There is no space in my head for anyone but Sally.

'Wait here,' says Mr Craven. 'I'll find Governor Jones and put a stop to this.'

'How long have we got?' I ask.

Mr Craven checks his watch. 'It's nine thirty. Please, try not to worry – there's still time.'

Ambrose asks if I am all right. I nod, but I'm not all right, not all right at all.

A blue vein throbs on Mr Emery's temple. 'How the deuce did that baying mob know?'

'Somehow word always gets out, Mr Emery,' replies Mr Craven. 'Stay here, all of you. I'll be back as soon as –'

A bell, low and hollow, sounds through the gaol. We grip each other, terrified.

'M-Mr Craven?' I stammer.

'It can't be.' Mr Craven checks his watch, over and over. He looks up, horrified. 'They're . . . early. They're starting early. Why? I don't unders–'

The door slams shut and there's a rattle of a key in the lock, then a crunching, scraping noise as we are locked in. A black shape behind the glass panel twists like a reflection in a house of mirrors, the flash of white at the neck unmistakable.

Reverend Silas Tate.

The bell tolls for a second time.

'It's probably best you stay in there,' Mr Tate says from behind the door. 'I suggested the governor get a move on and it's just as well, seeing as how you fools won't listen to reason. It won't take long. I've given the girl her last rites, not that she stopped blubbering long enough to listen.'

We are trapped. Fury boils up through me. 'You monster!' I scream. 'You evil, twisted monster!'

My scalp prickles. Something else is in here, with us.

Shadows tumble in, stealing into the corners of the room, but I ignore them – or at least I try to, but there are so many of them. *You're getting stronger,* Mr Bletchley said. I shudder.

'This is insanity, Tate. Open that door!' orders Mr Craven.

Then Mr Bletchley leaps forward, pressing his face to the glass. 'For pity's sake, Tate, this has gone far enough. Let us out of here! That girl is innocent! You know she is. You tried to blackmail me, and it seems that you have Governor Jones in your pocket as well!'

'Who, me?' replies Mr Tate, his face, strangely pale and luminescent, pressed up to the glass. 'I am a man of God. Who would believe your ramblings against my word?'

'Mr Tate, you are quite mad,' pronounces Mr Linworth as the vicar walks away. 'Is there any other way out, Mr Craven?'

'No,' says Mr Craven. 'If the vicar won't release us, we'll have to wait for the guards to do their rounds. That won't be until . . . after the execution.' The bell tolls once more. 'The hanging can't be stopped,' says Mr Craven, pacing the room. 'Even if the door would open, there's no time now!'

'NO!' I howl, and Cecily reels away from me, knocking into the table and sending the jug of water crashing to the floor. I fall to my knees, not caring about the shards of glass spiking into me, and, through my sobs, I feel her.

I look up.

She is here, the ghost girl, standing beside me. Not shimmering in and out of focus, but here and strong and ready. She holds the Book of Devona in her hands, outstretched, like an offering.

'Help me,' I beg, and she smiles.

'Together,' she whispers, 'we have to be together,' and suddenly I know. I know!

'Cecily, Oti, we have to join hands,' I say.

'No, we can't!' says Cecily, stricken.

Oti stands and walks to her, reaching out her hand. 'We must, Ceci.'

The three of us step away from the table. 'Ready?' I say.

We hold hands.

We all feel it, the crackle and jolt of energy. It pulses through us, draining us of ourselves, allowing them in. Immediately, there is movement, the room throbbing and vital; it is worse than before.

'I say, what on earth is happening?' says Mr Linworth to Bletchley. 'Is it part of the show?'

'No, you idiot,' snaps Bletchley.

We three girls cling together as the spirits grow ever more frantic, black souls pushing at the barrier between here and there. What can the others see? Do they see the shrieking shadows, the flesh-stripped limbs and bony jaws with needle-sharp teeth? Can they feel the rage? I hope not, for their sakes.

'More,' says the ghost girl, linking in between us. I can feel her, she is almost flesh, and from Oti's expression I know she feels her too. 'We need more of us,' says the girl.

'*Us?*'

'What's happening? What's going on in there? Is this another ridiculous performance?' spits Mr Tate. 'Enough of this poppycock!'

I can see him through the small window of the door, pressed against the wall, a shadow moving across his front, shifting its position to that of a babe in arms, seeking to suckle. I retch, metallic-tasting bile rising in my throat. Does the shadow recognize him as one of its own? Someone evil? The vicar clutches at his chest.

'Quickly!' I shout to the ghost girl. 'Who do you mean?'

'I think she means me.' Mr Bletchley steps towards us. 'She means me.'

'Really? I don't think –'

Oof!

The effect is instant, a lightning bolt through my body. The spirits fill the room, whirling and agitated, and the breeze picks up; hats are lifted and thrown, clothes are ruffled, hair is blown. The lamp is smashed and we are entirely in darkness, save for the glow of the ghost girl and the faint borrowed light through the door. The bell tolls again.

'More,' she says.

'Ambrose, come here, there's a good chap,' says Bletchley.

'What, me? No, I really don't think –'

'Ambrose, please! Now!'

There is no time to consider what this means; there are different shapes among the spectres as reedy threads solidify to form human outlines, imprints of men once contained within these walls.

The table shakes and shudders. 'Out of the way!' warns Mr Craven, as it flips and slams into the wall.

'We have to get out of here!' shouts Mr Linworth, banging at the door. 'Let us out, let us out! Someone, open the door!'

Outside, Tate slinks to the floor, where squealing creatures swarm and scuttle around him. 'Get off me!' he snarls, curling into himself.

'Please!' I yell at the ghost girl. 'It isn't enough! We're still in here and Sally is out there! What should we do?'

'More,' she says, and closes her eyes.

The glow that surrounds her builds and builds, the hazy light burning brighter and sharper until I can no longer look.

A flash of silver light.

An explosion of pure pain in my heart.

Another soul in our circle: a man, with a wise, kind face and eyes the mirror of mine.

'Pa?' I say, and he smiles. He is still looking out for me, in death, as he did in life.

It's five years since he passed.

Five years he's been holding on, resisting his burn.

Five years since the first accident in the pit.

Five years since Mr Tate dismissed my warning, vital moments lost, precious lives wasted.

Five years since I picked the wrong person to tell my secret to. If I had trusted someone else, my father might have lived.

It was my father who came to me, that day, drifting as he was between life and death. Somehow, he pulled himself back from the brink, only to die in Mama's arms as I mopped his brow not three days after they took his leg.

And it's my father who's here with me now.

'Hold on,' says Pa. 'This may get a little bumpy.'

It's hard to hear anything over the roar of the souls in the room: we seven cling together as if standing on a pier in the middle of a gale. The others huddle in a corner, shielded by the upturned table. I can no longer see Mr Tate's face through the glass of the door; he is entirely consumed by black, shredded creatures.

The human-formed spirits surround us, snarling like a pack of dogs baying for flesh. A growl comes out of the blackness and they thunder towards me, picking me out, but I stand firm.

I've met their like before.

'I know what you want!' I shout. 'You want me. Do it! Take me down with you. But first take me to the gallows! Cut Sally down! Or, so help me, I'll send you right back to hell to burn for all eternity!'

Snarling a terrible battle cry, a spirit throws back its head, its sinewy, chewed neck stretching and constricting like a concertina. But I stand strong, daring it.

'No, Peggy!' shouts Pa. 'They'll consume you!'

'I have to, Pa, I have to!'

I scream as the door bursts open as more phantoms surge through, splintering woodwork as they course through the room.

'What do we do?' shouts Ambrose, my fear reflected in his eyes.

And then, through the gale, I see them. They move through the maelstrom like the slow pull of the tide, certain and unstoppable – silhouetted at first, holding hands like paperchain dolls.

'Who are you?' I ask, but I know. *I know.*

Quickly they surround me, and it feels like home. These women and girls are my ancestors. I see the faces of Granny Vada, Cousin Frances, Aunt Kitty from the paintings on our cottage walls, and countless others who are strangers to me, and, yet, I know them. These women are Devonas. These women will help me.

Together.

'What do we do?' repeats Ambrose, and I grab his hand and shout.

'We run!'

Ribbons of energy are wrapping themselves in crackling, glowing strands round my limbs as I skitter through the prison like a leaf in a storm, at one point knocking me off my feet. I let go of Ambrose's hand. But my Devona sisters lift and push and power me on until – *WHOOSH!* – power crackles through my body like a firework.

'*Faster, faster!*' I shout as we cascade through corridors like a flash flood, the roar in my ears deafening me as we barrel into the courtyard and thunder towards the gallows, where a small figure in a grubby tunic, her hands bound behind her back, stumbles up the ladder to the platform.

Sally.

A white hood is shoved over her head.

'*Faster, please!*' I beg, and we push through the courtyard, kicking up dust and gathering dirt, knocking through the crowd as we gather speed.

The noose is placed round her neck.

There is a roar of hellish thunder from all around me and the dust cloud swallows the gallows from sight.

'No! Sally!' I scream, but the sound comes out as an unearthly growl.

For *we* are the storm, my sisters and I.

We are Devonas.

We are whisperlings.

'CUT HER DOWN!' I bellow.

And then: silence.

It's like I have stepped outside of myself.

'What *was* it?' says someone. 'That wind, that . . . noise? Was it . . . God?'

The mob surge forward again and, as we are jostled among them, I push through, released now from the careful clutches of my ancestors, elbowing my way to the front, heart squeezed dry in despair.

'Please, let me through, please!' Silence falls once again, like a sorrow-laden blanket, and suddenly the way is clear as the crowd step aside to make a path for me.

And then I see her, crumpled on the ground.

Oti is beside me. 'Quickly,' she says. She takes my hand, but I can't move; I don't want to see Sally like this.

'Come on, Peggy!' says Oti, face contorted in confusion. 'What are you waiting for?'

I don't understand.

And then, all of a sudden, I do. I look up, up, up through the trapdoor. The executioner is on his knees, sobbing. 'Did you hear it?' he's saying. 'That voice! Did you hear it? *Cut her down*, it said. Cut her down.'

A length of rope is curled on the dusty ground.

'Sally! Sally!' I scrabble through the dirt. Oti removes the noose from her neck, and I lift the hood. Her face is pale, crusted in dirt and streaked with tears; her waist-length hair has been shorn short like a boy's. I put an ear to her mouth to see if she's breathing; I can hear nothing but my own choked sobs. 'Sally, please!' I rest my forehead on her chest. 'Please.'

I slide my arms round her and pull her close, stroking her back and hugging her tight, pushing my face into her matted hair, rubbing my cheek against hers.

'Peggy? That you?' says a trembling, scratchy voice.

'Sally!' Relief floods every part of me. I sit back on my haunches and gather her to me, cradling her like a baby.

'Am I . . . am I on my burn, Peg?'

'No! No, Sal, no, you're fine, you're alive.'

'I . . . didn't do it, Peg. She was . . . good to me, she was getting more and more poorly . . . and then he came, again, insisted on having tea with her though she weren't up to it. And he left me with her when she started foamin' at the mouth. Oh, Peg, it were awful. I shouted for a doctor . . . I was there, holdin' her hand . . . and then he . . . he . . .' She dissolves into rasping sobs, her chest rattling and wheezy.

'I know, Sally, I know. It'll be all right now.' Mr Craven comes over as I soothe her, bringing blankets. I look up at him. 'It will be,' I ask, 'won't it?'

He nods tightly, sheeny, red-ringed eyes throwing a steely glare at Governor Jones, who cowers on the gallows platform, mouth covered by a handkerchief to shield himself from the stench from the docks and his shame from the crowd, whose mood has turned against him in the blowing of the mysterious wind. 'You have my word,' promises Mr Craven.

'We'll get to the seaside after all, Sal,' I whisper.

Sally smiles through cracked lips. 'You saved me,' she breathes. 'You an' your special gift. I'm sorry I called you an abominable-ation, Peg. You're not! You're my best friend.'

Cecily takes a blanket from Mr Craven, shakes it out and eases it round Sally's bird-like frame. 'Here, let's cover her up. Gently now . . . there we are.'

'Time to go,' I say, stroking Sally's short hair.

'It is,' says a voice that comes from both far away and deep in my heart.

'Pa?' I turn to look. Pa is here, the glow around him so luminous that I can barely look. 'No, Pa, please don't go!'

'I have to, Peg. I've waited as long as I can.' He smiles and glances upwards. 'Pushed my luck a bit, truth be told. Hope I'm not in trouble with anyone.'

Mr Bletchley stands close by. He removes his hat and holds it to his chest. He is crying. My father addresses him: 'Keep an eye on her for me, brother.' Then Pa turns to me, smiling. 'You were right, Peg, I should have let you read the book. The key is under the brass rabbit. I'm so sorry I didn't want you to have it before. From now on you must do it your way.'

'It doesn't matter, Pa – I don't care,' I say. 'Please don't go!'

'I love you, Peg, and I'm so very proud of you. Tell your ma that –'

'You can tell me yourself, John.'

'Mama!' I throw myself at her, hugging her close, breathing her in. My brave, wonderful, fierce mother.

'*Peachy?*' says Pa. 'You . . . you can see me?'

Mama nods, tears streaming down her face. 'I can! I may not have been able to before, John, but you've always been there – in everything I see, in everyone I love,' she says, smiling at me.

'My girls,' says Pa. 'My loves. My life.' He reaches out and strokes my cheek and I can feel it, an imprint of his love left by the softest breeze.

The radiance that gently haloed Pa for five years burns brighter and brighter, shining gossamer threads layering and aligning until ablaze.

And then he's gone.

Pa won't come back, not this time. Sadness barrels into my chest and I feel full and empty, all at once.

He's gone. I want to fall to my knees and scream and beg for his return.

This must be how Mama has felt all along. Sensing him, but not seeing him. I squeeze her tightly. We stand there, holding each other up for a good long while until she kisses my cheek, says something about helping Sally inside, to come along as it's getting cold, and let's get away from this hateful place.

As Mama moves away, I immediately feel another presence by my side. It's the ghost girl. Except she's not a ghost; she is completely here, and I can speak to her as easily as with anyone. There is a mark on her wrist, an etching like a sailor might have – not a naked lady or an anchor, but an outline of something vaguely familiar that I'm too exhausted to pinpoint.

'I'm really sorry about your dad,' she says. I can't trust myself to answer without bursting into tears, so I just nod. 'We really do look alike, don't we, you and me?' She peers at me. 'Sludge-coloured eyes and all . . . I don't have long,' she says, 'but I thought you may have a few questions.'

'One or two, yes.'

She smiles at me. 'I suppose the first thing to say is that we're related, way down the line. But I think you've guessed that by now. And I'm not really a ghost.'

'You . . . aren't?' I don't understand, although it would explain why she is like no other spirit that I have met.

'It's confusing, I know. I mean, I'm not a ghost here, where I am, like you're not a ghost there, where you are. I think it's because we're both direct from the Devona bloodline, which makes our whisperling abilities really strong. Those incredible spirits of women and girls who helped you today? They're from the past – hundreds, thousands of years, even. And I'm from the future. You're the whisperling now and I'm it . . . later on. We're all linked, through time, somehow. Perhaps we'll find out for sure and that'll be our chapter to write in the book.' Her voice is getting thinner and the flickering has begun. 'You are a pure whisperling, Peggy, the strongest in your time. But sometimes even the chosen Devona girls need help. We're here if you need us. And the others, of course.'

'Others?'

'Yes! We're all over the place once you start looking. Not so many direct descendants like you and me, but the bloodline runs far and wide. Together, we are stronger.'

Bloodline? My mind goes to the parchment on Mr Bletchley's study floor. Could it have been a family tree?

'What's your name?' I can hardly see her any more, my whisperling descendant from the future.

'Meg. My name is Meg. Named after you.'

'Oh! That's lovely! Goodbye, Meg.'

'Keep the book safe!' she tells me. 'They'll do anything to get it!'

They?

But she's gone.

30

We move inside to the governor's office. A doctor is called to examine Sally, and I step into the corridor for a moment, alone, numb with grief for Pa, but heady with relief for Sally. I don't know which to feel first.

Mr Tate's lifeless body lies discarded, a shrunken, shrivelled husk. 'He's dead,' says the prison doctor. 'Heart attack, by the looks of things.'

'Good,' I say.

The doctor raises an eyebrow. 'I'll see to the others. There's nothing that can be done for him.'

I step over Mr Tate's body, empty and finished and silent. The same thing can't be said, however, for his spirit, which has jibber-jabbered in my ear since the moment I got here.

'Get back here, girl!' Spirit Tate looms closer, even more twisted and ugly in death than in life: features flint sharp, eyes bulbous, black robes writhing as if alive with vermin. His white collar is bloodstained and knot-tight, digging into his neck.

'You pathetic, evil little man!' I shout. 'You would have had Sally hanged for *money*? You would have had me thrown into Bedlam, painting me as mad so as to discredit anything I said about you, anything the dead told me about you, for *money*?' I shake my head. 'Enough. Enough of you.'

'Do you really think this was about money, you silly girl? That was only half of it! Don't you realize? You're an abomination, Peggy Devona. I've spent my life trying to rid this earth of ungodly creatures like you. And don't think I'm alone in that mission – there are plenty of us out there waiting to crush you and your kind. Sally was merely my bait.'

Bait? I glance round, see no one, and aim a sharp kick at his side. 'You are one of The Righteous, aren't you?'

'I *am* The Righteous!' he replies. 'I started it – it is *my* organization. And we are everywhere.' His edges are the black and red of burning embers; something bad is coming for him. I watch in silent awe as the shadows crawl towards him. He flicks and flaps at something black and insect-like on his arm. 'What are these creatures upon me?' He reaches towards me but snaps back like a wishbone, scuttling beasts swarming up his legs and chest. 'They're biting!'

'You can't stay here, Silas. It's time to leave.'

'Your precious father stayed!'

I pull myself up to my full height. 'My father was a Devona.' My voice catches. I'm not used to speaking of Pa in the past tense. 'And you, Silas, are not.'

I walk back into the governor's office, leaving Silas Tate to his doom. Pulling the door closed, I slump against it, exhausted.

'Everything . . . all right?' asks Ambrose, regarding me with concern.

'It is now, I think.' I hope. 'So . . . are we related? You, Cecily, Oti – all of us?' I ask.

He nods. 'Not Cecily, but the rest of us, yes. Extremely loosely, but that doesn't appear to matter. And there was me thinking that I'd gained my employment by virtue of my ability and reputation, when all along it was because of nepotism.'

'But . . . you two, you're men,' I say. 'I thought it was just the women . . .'

'Oh, goodness me, yes, we men are of no use at all alone.' Mr Bletchley steps forward. 'Tonight was an exception, more a question of quantity than quality.' He smiles. 'But you're absolutely right. We are all Devonas,' he says.

'*We are all Devonas*,' I parrot, astounded. 'The parchment, in your office . . .'

'All part of the research. It struck me that I only knew of whisperlings from the Devona line, and I thought that, perhaps, if I found more Devonas, I might find more whisperlings.'

'To staff your emporiums?'

He fidgets uncomfortably. 'Initially, maybe that *was* my idea, yes. But then . . . it became more of a quest to replace the family I thought I'd lost forever. I appreciate it was risky bringing Ambrose into the fold as well, considering his links to you, but frankly his father is an ass and I wanted to help. Oti, I traced through the family tree. Cecily, on the other hand, I can't explain.' He looks over at her and Oti, who crouch on the floor, hands fiercely laced as if stopping the other from drowning. He shrugs. 'Maybe family is not made by blood alone. Perhaps love is enough.'

'Perhaps.' I rub the bandaged burn on my wrist and Mr Bletchley regards me with concern. 'You should let the doctor treat that while he's here. I'm sorry, by the way.'

I look at him for a moment, then I understand. 'The scalding poker – it made me break the chain. Was . . . was that you? How did you know what was happening? And what to do?'

He raises an eyebrow and says, 'Well, I have learned certain things, being a Devona. I did pay some attention to the whole whisperling business, you know.' And, with that, he pulls his shoulders back, with an uppity expression on his face that I've seen a million times in my own mirror.

'I forgive you, Mist– Uncle Jed,' I say awkwardly.

Uncle Jed wipes away a tear and, for the first time in days, I smile.

It's late November, almost two months since the events at Spike Island. Clifton Lodge glints in the frosty sunshine, its slate roof sparkling as if sprinkled with icing sugar. Sally is collecting a few of her belongings before we make the journey back to Alderley together to visit our families. Next year, I shall be returning to Bristol, and to school.

Cecily and Oti can't wait. Although they are not much more than six years older than me, they are to be my 'town parents' and have purchased a giddying array of aprons and insisted that Mrs Morris teach them to bake because, according to Cecily, 'It's what mothers do, which is gurt lush, innit?' Cecily has embraced her natural accent because, she says, it is important to be your true self – and who am I to argue with that?

'*It's what mothers do.*' I smile at this, thinking of the many other things my particular mother does – keeping a family afloat emotionally and economically, crusading against injustice, protecting a secret supernatural legacy . . . but I don't want to put them off. They're very enthusiastic, and I love them both. Oti's whisperling skills are developing too – something definitely happened on the night of the seance that boosted the abilities of us all. Well, of us girls, at least. Much to Ambrose's relief, he's the same as he was before.

The Lodge will be kept in trust for Sally until she is of age. Lady Stanton set out in her will that all her staff should benefit from her fortune, and Sally is determined to do right by them.

The staff are leasing Clifton Lodge to Mr and Mrs Craven, who have proved useful and fearless allies in the complicated, but ultimately successful, clearing of Sally's name and reinstating of Lady Stanton's will. They have also convicted Mr Tate of Lady Stanton's murder, even though he's dead. We have heard no more from The Righteous; I hope Silas Tate's crusade against whisperlings was but one man's deadly obsession. Sally's parents and George are staying in the family cottage for now, although it has been much improved. Needless to say, little George's chimney-sweeping days are over.

There have been other changes too.

'I never trusted that weasel-faced old goat,' whispers Lady Stanton, fluttering through the hall as I wait for Sally to pack her things. 'That a vicar should have framed poor Sally for his own crime, coming here dropping poison into my tea every day! Oh, the devious swine! The *monster*! I still regret not being able to tell you more when you came to the house that day, Margaret my dear. I was halfway across realms, you see.' I'm not sure what that means, yet, but I'm sure I'll find out in time.

'Thank you for seeing me now, though, Lady Stanton. I know it isn't easy.'

'You're more than welcome, my dear. You're quite a draw, you know. We can all see you, all of us, from wherever we are, however far along we've got on our final journey. I've received I don't know how many envious looks ever since you asked to see me.' She flits and floats, like a will-o'-the-wisp, darting this way and that, a sparky flash of energy.

'My late husband is over here somewhere, you know,' she tells me. 'I'm going to try and find him if I can. Do you think that's possible, Margaret dear?'

'I hope so, Lady Stanton,' I say, thinking of my father, and Bertie. 'I really do.' Or perhaps, like Mrs Morris, they could find their way back if they want to.

We trundle back to Alderley, Sally and I, huddled under a nest of blankets in the carriage Mr Craven has lent us. Sally's head is on my shoulder, red curls tickling my nose. Her hair is still short, but it is glossy from being washed and brushed. She has taken to winding it in papers overnight for 'a wave'. It's fashionably risqué, according to Cecily, and I must say I rather like it.

'Ooh, shall we have a lardy for later, Peg? My treat.'

'All right, Your Highness, no need to show off,' I tease, shoving her good-naturedly. 'Drop me off at the baker's. You go and see your folks and I'll bring the cake up.'

Her lightness of mood is a relief and a layer of worry peels away and floats from my shoulders. Although she didn't spend another night in that place, it was a different Sally that came back from the gaol, a Sally who fears the dark, and still suffers terrible nightmares and is quick to flinch at sudden movement.

It will take time, says Oti, and kindness.

33

There is much kindness in Alderley for Sally, and me too now, for that matter. All the posters have gone and there is a comforting sense of utter indifference about whisperlings, which I'm hugely grateful for. That afternoon when Sally and I arrived in the village, I tucked the sticky package from the baker's into my basket ('Have a couple on the house,' said Mr Sweeting, 'and tell that poor girl we're thinking of her') and headed up the hill to home.

Even Mrs Dulwich, the chemist, rushed out to give me a tiny stoppered bottle. 'A tincture for Sally's nerves,' she said – comfrey, poppy, yarrow and nasturtium – one drop only or she'd be seeing double. 'I tried to keep an eye on you,' she added, her black cat winding around her feet. 'I couldn't bear the thought of all that creeper nonsense starting up again. But they're good folk round here and they look out for their own. Now they're used to it, they won't let you come to any harm, don't you worry.'

Since I've been home, Mrs Dulwich has fed me her life story bit by bit, the distress of it all too great to be told in one sitting. This woman, who herself survived the scorch of suspicion, only wanted to protect me. How did I not see it before? In the old days, Mrs Dulwich would have been burned at the stake for the herbs she grows in her garden, and yet here she is, making potions in plain sight and no one so much as blinks an eye, her skills legitimized now that she practises them from her chemist's shop. *Yes*, I think, *she's right. They're used to it* . . .

Mrs Dulwich wasn't the only surprise – it turns out that there were many things I missed. Like how Uncle Jed (I am slowly getting used to this) funded his research into the Devona family tree by selling his belongings – his silverware, antiques and paintings – and reducing his housekeeping staff to one. One Devona, in fact, albeit a cousin many,

many times removed. When he told me, I almost wet myself.

'So Dotty is a whisperling?' I spluttered.

'Well, no, she's a Devona, very distantly –'

'So she could be a whisperling?'

'I don't think –'

'But she could be?'

'Peggy –'

'Can I tell her?'

'Stop it.'

'Can I, though, please?'

'No . . . Yes . . . Oh dash it, do as you wish!'

Poor Dotty. After her dramatic appearance at the seance, an unseen hand shoved her into the water closet and locked the door from the outside. *Hours* she was in there before she was released, babbling about ghouls and poltergeists and flying pheasants and how 'that old crone' had never left. A suitable punishment is yet to be decided, but Sally is keen to have her come and work at the Lodge so she can keep an eye on her. I think she feels sorry for her, duped and brainwashed as she was by Mr Tate. I agree with Sally. What harm can it do?

'Oh dear, I can't imagine why Dotty was so disagreeable!' Mama commented sarcastically when Uncle Jed told her that he hadn't replaced Mrs Morris after she'd died. 'When I think of poor Dotty running that huge house all by herself for all those months – why ever would she *possibly* want to believe in someone promising to make her rich?'

Uncle Jed couldn't understand it either, having raised her salary, he said, by 'a farthing' and given her every Thursday afternoon off as well.

'Oh, *men!*' cried Mama in exasperation, as Uncle Jed ducked to avoid the *thwack* from her tea-towel that pinged his hat clean off.

It is good to be home. The kitchen is gloriously warm, and the rich, round smell of bread baking in the oven and drop scones browning on the hotplate floods my senses with love. Uncle Jed is here and keen to know how Sally is doing.

'Threatening to change the name of the Lodge to Hubbard House,' I tell him, 'but other than that she seems to be handling it well. She's talking about setting up a charity, for those who need legal help and can't afford it.'

Uncle Jed smiles. 'Fighting injustice on behalf of those who don't usually have a voice. Very good, Sally. Very good indeed.'

'Mr Linworth, the magistrate, is advising her. I think he still feels guilty for not realizing Tate was a wrong 'un.'

'He's not alone in his guilt, Peggy. Many should have realized he was a rotten apple, myself included.'

Mama pats him on the shoulder affectionately, and a pang of loyalty to Pa stabs my heart for a moment. But then, it is only as it should be; we are family, after all. The new silver-framed picture on the sideboard attests to this – a copy of the mysterious disappearing photograph from Mr Bletchley's house. In the photo, my mother wears the dark-blue dress that I'd taken with me to Bristol; little wonder it troubled Uncle Jed so to see me wearing it at our final seance.

I've learned since that the photographs on the landing wall at number seven Beckford Square are portraits of Devonas from far and wide. The tiny smudges of light I saw are signs of the whisperling gift within an individual, and visible only to others that have it. Uncle Jed once hoped to use his camera to catch ghosts in his photographs; he may have failed at that, but unintentionally captured so much more.

The day our silver-framed photograph was taken, it was Pa who was behind the camera. He took it just days before Mama chose him as her husband, and the brothers' falling-out began. They both loved her – and both still do, I can see that now. I can also see that Mama had made her choice long before the photograph was taken, for the glow on the image shines from behind her tummy, where I am.

This is information that I'll likely keep to myself, for now at least.

A photo of Pa from the Beckford Square collection stands next to Mama and Uncle Jed on the sideboard, the three friends finally reunited. And the navy-blue business card of the Psychic Emporium rests against the brass rabbit, keeping its eye on us all.

EPILOGUE

The key was hidden under the brass rabbit, as Pa said. The box opens easily and I lift the book from its velvet bed and place it in front of me on the parlour floor, running my fingers over the old leather.

'Meg told me to keep you safe,' I whisper. 'I will, I promise.'

I pause, pressing both palms flat against the cover, and close my eyes. Energy roars in my ears as a thousand faces flash before my eyes and I fall back, as if a surge of electricity has knocked me over.

I'm not scared. These are not spirits sent to torment me. These are my Devona sisters, here for each other.

Past, present . . . future. Stronger, *together*. Enriching each other. Teaching each other.

And so now it's finally my turn to write in the Book of Devona, transcribing pages from my own journal to pass on my knowledge to the next girl who has the gift.

Don't be scared, I begin.

They surround us. They are as much part of this life as the elements. They are the breeze that brushes your cheek, the first call of birdsong, the shimmer of heat from the sun. They are in the empty chair in your parlour, that spare seat in your hansom cab. They are under your bed.

That movement in the gloom? It is them.

Unexplained creaks, mysterious footsteps? Them.

The shiver on your neck that causes you to turn?

The time you thought yourself not quite alone?

You weren't. They are always here, close by, watching. Waiting.

Don't be scared.

I run my fingers over the page.

Wait. It isn't lumpen and damp-swelled.

It's embossed.

I grab a pencil, shading and smudging it with my fingertips. And then I look at the page again, and I laugh and laugh.

It's a symbol.

An eye, set in front of a crown, exactly like the illustration on Mr Bletchley's business card. Except it isn't a crown. The markings in the book are far more intricate, far more . . . alive. A flicker of heat rises up from the page.

It isn't a crown. It's a flame. An eye and a flame.

The mark Meg had on her wrist. The mark of Devona.

For those that see the burn.

A NOTE FROM
THE AUTHOR

Dear Reader,

I hope you enjoyed Peggy and Sally's story! If I could keep you for another minute, I'd love to tell you a bit about some of the real-life inspirations behind my book.

I was messing about on the internet, pretending to write the (appalling!) first draft of *The Whisperling*, when I came across the story of a seventeen-year-old girl, Sarah Harriet Thomas, who had been sent to the gallows in the mid nineteenth century for the murder of her mistress.

Not only that, years before Sarah's case, Susannah Underwood was hanged at Gloucester on Friday, 19 April 1776, for setting fire to a barn and a haystack. A newspaper at the time criticized the 'bad manners of the girl' for refusing to shake hands with her master at her execution. She was fifteen.

The true stories of these young girls, and others like them, got me thinking. Did they have anyone to speak for them at their trials? Was anyone on *their* side? And would it have made a difference if they'd come from wealthy families instead of poor ones?

I had already invented the story of Peggy and her family – and, from the inspiration of Sarah and Susannah's sad ends, the character of Peggy's best friend, Sally Hubbard, came to life. Granted, their tales are quite different – Sarah had indeed bashed her mistress's brains in with a boulder – but both Sarah and Sally (and indeed Susannah) were from poor backgrounds, and with no one willing to help them they were voiceless young women whom the brutal legal system was utterly against.

It has forever been so.

With Sarah and Susannah in mind, I wanted to write a positive ending for Sally. I've taken some artistic licence with dates (although teenagers truly were victims of capital punishment until as late as 1932), but the awful way children were treated throughout the Victorian era – for example, children working as chimney sweeps when they were barely out of nappies – is astonishing. I wanted to explore just some of this in *The Whisperling*, though an entire story about a chimney sweep's apprentice would have been far too bleak, even for my tastes.

I also wanted to acknowledge the freemining tradition of the Forest of Dean, where I grew up. It was a dangerous way to make a living and, again, children as young as eight or nine were regularly sent down into the dark to work. The mining accident in the book is a fictionalized account of an all-too-frequent tragedy. Should you ever visit the Forest of Dean – and you should, for it is beautiful – you will find nestled among the trees and the cycle paths and walking trails, numerous sculptures and memorials: important reminders of a legacy that shaped the landscape and the people in it.

The Whisperling is, of course, a work of fiction and there is a mixture of the real and unreal throughout: Spike Island, for example, was the home of the British New Gaol until 1849, but it is *such* a good name I had to use it for my story; Alderley is a made-up village very loosely based on Tintern, in the Wye Valley. Geography wasn't my strong point at school (nor indeed were any other fact-based subjects), so please forgive me if my knowledge of topography sucks. I was good at English, though it's probably lucky (although my editors would likely disagree) that my generation didn't get taught anything more complicated than basic grammar ('A subordinate clause? What is that? One of Santa's helpers? Ho, ho, HO!') as I would have likely sucked at that, too.

The Colston statue, however – the one with the dolphins Peggy sees in Bristol – is a very real (if now upended) thing. It was erected in 1895, two years before the book is set, and torn down in 2020, the year I finished the first draft. Edward Colston, the man on whom the statue was based, became rich and famous in the seventeenth century because he was involved in the buying of people from Africa and selling them to America as slaves. It is documented that there was little public support for the Colston statue right from the off, and raising funds for it had been challenging. This cheers me.

It is unimaginable now to think of celebrating anyone who profits from human suffering, and to redress the balance in some small way I named Beckford Square in my story after Carmen Beckford, an iconic Bristol woman who campaigned tirelessly to improve racial equality in the city. I read about so many inspirational people while choosing the name, and no doubt there are many, many more whose names and contributions will never be known. I am thankful there are good people everywhere, and that the Reverend Silas Tates of this world are outnumbered, for sure.

And, finally, as for whether whisperlings are real or not . . . Well, we know the answer to that, don't we . . . ?

Hxx

ACKNOWLEDGEMENTS

Where to start . . .? The incredible team at Puffin, who, without exception, are wonderful. I don't know what I expected (Puffin are, after all, A Big Deal), but I am extremely thankful that Peggy found her home here.

Special mention to my amazing editor and chief cheerleader, Katie Sinfield – thank you for making me feel never less than entirely supported and nurtured. I can't imagine a better fit. It has been a joy working with you and I've loved every minute. Please can we do it again? And again and again! Wendy Shakespeare for her incredible precision and kindness, and Sarah Hall, Petra Bryce and Laura Dean for their astonishingly sharp eyes.

The Whisperling shines because of you all. #TeamWhisperlingForever

Designer Emily Smyth for her magical art direction (Sally's letter is the coolest thing ever), and the incredible artistry of Kristina Kister, who somehow reached into my brain, plucked out my vision of the whisperling world, squished it on to the cover and made it astonishingly beautiful.

My agent, Megan Carroll – she with all the questions. I was one of her first clients and it feels like we've grown together (although she is still very young and I am old, which is extraordinarily unfair and confusing). I will be forever in your debt and will consequently be sending you giant bottles of wine until the day I die. We did it!

My amazing writing family:

Amanda Reynolds and Kate Riordan, whose friendship is everything. Couldn't have done it without you ladies and would certainly be enjoying it far less.

Helen Maslin, who was there at the very beginning, when our children were wee and writing a book was a thing we spoke about in dreamy, abstract terms at the school gates. Judith Green, Loraine Evans, Henri Smethurst-McIntyre, who played early, critical roles. Jane Bailey, who my traitor of a dog loves more than me, and the wider group of Cotswold writers for allowing me into the gang in spite of being unpublished and suffering from major imposter syndrome.

The online writing community, in particular both the supportive and generous #Debut22 Twitter groups I'm part of. This may be the year we get to change our header: #TeamForeverUnannounced!

I am very lucky to have the most incredible group of friends, some writers, some not. I daren't name names for fear of missing someone out, which would haunt me forever, but special mention goes to Tracy for producing two early readers in the shape of my god-daughters, and to Toni for being a little drop of magic and the most inspirational woman I know. Love you to the moon and back.

To my family:

The Olds who are embarrassingly proud (profound apologies to all booksellers who have encountered Kathy Fisher banging on about her daughter's book that she 'can't talk about because it's a secret'. Not any more – go Mum!)

Ollie, my lovely boy, from whom I occasionally get an encouraging pat on the head, and to his brothers who are grown and flown, meaning there is now space for me to have an office. ☺

The World's Best Husband™, Steve, for quietly turning a blind eye at my lacklustre jobhunting efforts when I was made redundant. This book is for you, my love. K&B may have pipped you to the post for the dedication, on account of their seniority, but, yes, you can now take early retirement . . . in about five to seven years (that's publishing!).

And, finally, to the person holding this book in their hands. A thousand times, thank you.

A Q&A WITH
HAYLEY HOSKINS

How did you come up with the idea of whisperlings?

That's an interesting question! Whisperlings – those who can talk to the dead – was a concept I first wrote about many years ago, in a different book that has not (yet!) been published. It interested me so much that I created a whole world around it.

As a kid I was obsessed with weird things that seemed 'real' – the Cottingley Fairies, the Enfield Hauntings, the Amityville Horror. Even when they were proved to be untrue, I'd think, *Yeah, but what if . . . ?*

These supernatural stories were told against backdrops of complete normality, like, *Yeah, you may be chilling with the undead, but you still have to get up for school or work*, and I love that vibe. *Buffy the Vampire Slayer* is the OG inspiration, of course. The BBC TV series *Being Human* (set in Bristol!) is another example. I also have a major passion for creepy gothic books, so I squished all this together in my brain and came up with Peggy and the whisperling legacy.

Do you have a favourite character?

Oh, wow, you *really* want me to choose? Peggy, of course, but other than her I would probably say Ambrose. He is good and kind and totally out of his depth, but keen to help and do the right thing. I don't have a brother but I'd very much like one like him (even if he is an annoying fopdoodle!). ☺

If you had whisperling abilities, whose ghost would you like to speak with?

I'd start with Mary Shelley, I think. She wrote *Frankenstein* when she was a teenager, which is an astonishing feat, and her life was fascinating, though not always in a good way. I'd also like to speak to whoever designed Stonehenge, because I have *questions*. Oh, and my nan – Vada Matilda Frances Dowle – who would have *loved* whisperlings.

Were there any books that inspired y ou to write this story?

In terms of adult books, Sarah Waters' *Affinity* is definitely top of this list, as well as Laura Purcell's *The Silent Companions* and Frances Hardinge's *The Lie Tree*. And then for children's books, Jacqueline Wilson's *Hetty Feather*, Eloise Williams' *Gaslight* – all amazing stories about young women having odd experiences and doing extraordinary things in stuffy, buttoned-up times.

Were there any challenges in writing the story?

Many! *The Whisperling* is the first historical fiction I've written – I'm very much a contemporary writer – and it's been an education, for sure. But I thought it would be so interesting to see how a character like Peggy would stand out against a rigid, old-fashioned setting. It's been great, though I hadn't realized how much time I'd spend googling things like 'did Victorians have chewing gum' or 'how did Victorian women deal with periods' (they simply didn't have them, as far as I can tell!). Also, I wanted the language to be easy to read but still feel authentically Victorian, which was tricky.

Which was your favourite part of *The Whisperling* to write?

The scenes with Oti and Cecily; they are so fun and cool, and I loved researching and describing their outfits! I wish they were my friends in real life. Honestly, I would love to do a spin-off where I follow them around when they're out and about, like a *Made in Chelsea*/*TOWIE* sort of reality show, but in Victorian times. Imagine! Ooh – and what if they time-travelled to present day? Quick, get my notepad!

I also enjoyed writing the scenes where I describe ghosts or spooky happenings; I love all that stuff. And if I write something that actually makes *me* cry – Bertie's death, for example – then that's a real moment for me too.

What is your writing process like?

Process? HahaHA!

It depends, really. I might read about something fascinating – for example, teenage capital punishment in Victorian England (cheery!) – and then I research everything I can find out about that subject until something pings in my head and I think, *Aha! Here is the most interesting bit! Here is my angle!* Or it might be a character, like Peggy, that I fall in love with and want to see how they would react in certain situations. For example, I knew I wanted to set *The Whisperling* in Victorian times, and it would be about a girl who has the gift of speaking with the dead, and then I found out how obsessed the Victorians were with spiritualism and *boom* – I was off!

It might sound weird, but when you first sit down to write something new it often feels like you're just making stuff up (I KNOW), and you may feel really self-conscious: *Oh, look here, I am doing writing!* But then you get into the characters and can see them doing their thing, and it feels less abstract, less weird. It takes a while for me to get to that point, but the only way to do it is to show up and crack on. So that is my advice. Show up and crack on.

Which books did you enjoy reading as a child?

So many! The earliest book I can remember loving is *The Magic Faraway Tree* by Enid Blyton, but my tweenage years were dominated by anything spooky. *The Wolves of Willoughby Chase* series by Joan Aitkin was an absolute favourite (I have ordered it to re-read, in fact). *Moondial* by Helen Cresswell is wonderful (ghosts, time travel, friendship – oh yes!). I also loved *Ginnie and the Mystery House* by Catherine Woolley and *Scary Stories to Tell in the Dark* by Alvin Schwartz. Oh! And *The World of the Unknown: Ghosts* was a constant companion, just to throw in a bit of non-fiction!

Which children's books do you wish you could have had on your shelf when you were young?

If I'd had access to the children's writers who inspire me today, I would have never left the house!

Jacqueline Wilson is the absolute queen – no topic is off limits and I love that. Louise Rennison was awesome (writing funny isn't easy!) and her *Angus, Thongs* series is something I would love to emulate one day – proper, laugh-out-loud stuff. Malorie Blackman, Frances Hardinge and Robin Stevens are all huge inspirations. Sarah Crossan is incredible (if you haven't read *One*, then please do, immediately – it's the ultimate writing lesson in how to make every word count). Emma Carroll, Maz Evans, Maria Kuzniar, Sharna Jackson . . . I could go on!

Also, I'm lucky enough to belong to a wonderful Twitter group of debut children's writers, and there are so many brilliant books coming your way – you are going to be spoiled, my friends!

If you weren't an author, what job would you like to do?

Well, I didn't go to university but came very close to applying to study journalism. It's difficult to call it a regret though, as who knows what I may have missed out on if I had gone down that path. I have been an estate agent, holistic therapist, customer-service supervisor, bank worker, jewellery-shop assistant and a receptionist among other things (and unless I sell a bajillion books there is every chance I will be one of those things again).

However, if we're talking about a *dream* life: I'd start my journalistic career, exposing injustices and winning many, many awards, and then lean into my love of Instagram hair and make-up tutorials and become a beauty journalist, if only for the free samples!

Are you working on any new books?

Always! I have a million ideas, all the time. I love writing funny stuff, so I could do a future book that's pure LOLs (with a bit of darkness and maybe a ghost or two, because, well, of course). At the moment, though, I'm writing another book in the whisperling universe, set against the backdrop of the First World War. I'd love to do a series of books about whisperlings, moving through time and ending up with a very modern (maybe slightly futuristic?) finale, where whisperlings save the universe!

ABOUT THE AUTHOR

Hayley Hoskins writes historical and contemporary young-adult and middle-grade fiction, and she loves anything a bit dark and gloomy and scary and funny.

Although first published at the age of twenty-one, it was getting longlisted for the Bath Children's Novel Award in 2015 that made Hayley believe that maybe she could do this writing thing full-time, and subsequently she has thrown out all her office clothes.

She dips into the sea whenever possible, so let's say 'wild swimming' is her favourite hobby. She spends as much time as she can with her wonderful friends – some of whom are writers, some not; as an only child, it delights her that in adulthood she has gathered a joyful amount of sisters.

Originally from the Forest of Dean, Hayley lives with her family and hairy breeze block of a dog in Cheltenham, Gloucestershire.

Follow Hayley on Twitter
@HayleyHoskins
#TheWhisperling

Q. Which book makes you laugh the most?

A. A very hard question to answer. The last book that made me seriously laugh out loud was Australian comic crime writer Shane Maloney's novel *Sucked In*. One could die laughing over Maloney's sex scenes with their ingenious double-entendres. Mil Millington's *Things My Girlfriend and I Have Argued About* is also painfully funny. And on an entirely different scale of amusement rating, I have to say that Vladimir Nabokov's *Lolita* is a novel I always read with a smile on my face, which despite its awful subject matter is endlessly jocular in a dense, allusive and literary way.

Q. If you had a friend who was ill, which book would you give them?

A. *As I Lay Dying?* Most of my friends share my twisted sense of humour ...

Q. If you were in a book club, which book would you introduce?

A. If I were in a book club it would be a disastrously one-sided affair in which I insisted on pressing upon the other members all my favourite titles. I would start with Flaubert's *Madame Bovary*, go on to Emily Bronte's *Wuthering Heights*, insist upon lingering in Charlotte Bronte's *Villette*, detour into Gogol's story *The Overcoat*, travel across to Gabriel Garcia Marquez's *Chronicle of a Death Foretold*, return to Kafka's *Metamorphosis*, then land for a while in *Lolita* of course, before heading south to some great Australian titles such as Thea Astley's *It's Raining in Mango*, Glenda Adams's *Dancing on Coral* and Gerald Murnane's *The Plains* ... and that's not even taking into account more recent titles such as Ann Patchett's *Bel Canto*, Carol Shields's *Unless* or anything by James Lee Burke. You can see why I'm not in a book club.

Reading Group Notes

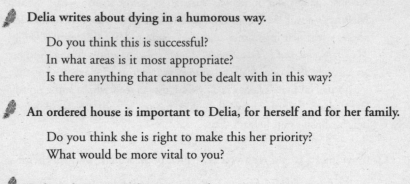

Delia writes about dying in a humorous way.

> Do you think this is successful?
> In what areas is it most appropriate?
> Is there anything that cannot be dealt with in this way?

An ordered house is important to Delia, for herself and for her family.

> Do you think she is right to make this her priority?
> What would be more vital to you?

Delia is keen to set the past to rights.

> Do you feel she manages to do so?
> Is it a realistic aim?

What makes a good mother?

> Is Delia one?
> Is Jean?

Delia writes advice for the living and for the dying.

> Do you find any of her practical suggestions useful?

Throughout, there are references to music of very different sorts.

> How much did this add to the novel?
> What music might you listen to if very ill?

Even more important to Delia is her love of reading.

> What books would you want to have around you under similar
> circumstances?
> What do you think of her choices?